PICK A FIGHT

Fargo did not much care for mistreating women and horses. A good horse, in his opinion, was more than an animal; it was a friend. To see a horse abused always rankled him. As for women, he was no knight in shining armor, but when one was being treated as Tilly was being treated, it made him want to stomp the prospector into the ground, preferably with a few teeth kicked in. So Fargo had plenty of motivation to do what he did next—namely, launch his fist from his hip and catch Stein flush on the jaw. For most that was enough. Fargo was big and he was rawhide tough. One punch would lay a man out as cold as ice.

But Stein had an iron jaw. Hitting it was like hitting an anvil. Stein staggered against another table and had to brace himself to stay on his feet, but he did not go down. Instead, shaking his head to clear it, he hefted his pick and straightened.

"Mister, you just brought yourself a whole heap of trouble."

THE
TRAILSMAN
#322

APACHE
AMBUSH

by

Jon Sharpe

A SIGNET BOOK

SIGNET
Published by New American Library, a division of
Penguin Group (USA) Inc., 375 Hudson Street,
New York, New York 10014, USA
Penguin Group (Canada), 90 Eglinton Avenue East, Suite 700, Toronto,
Ontario M4P 2Y3, Canada (a division of Pearson Penguin Canada Inc.)
Penguin Books Ltd., 80 Strand, London WC2R 0RL, England
Penguin Ireland, 25 St. Stephen's Green, Dublin 2,
Ireland (a division of Penguin Books Ltd.)
Penguin Group (Australia), 250 Camberwell Road, Camberwell, Victoria 3124,
Australia (a division of Pearson Australia Group Pty. Ltd.)
Penguin Books India Pvt. Ltd., 11 Community Centre, Panchsheel Park,
New Delhi - 110 017, India
Penguin Group (NZ), 67 Apollo Drive, Rosedale, North Shore 0632,
New Zealand (a division of Pearson New Zealand Ltd.)
Penguin Books (South Africa) (Pty.) Ltd., 24 Sturdee Avenue,
Rosebank, Johannesburg 2196, South Africa

Penguin Books Ltd., Registered Offices:
80 Strand, London WC2R 0RL, England

First published by Signet, an imprint of New American Library,
a division of Penguin Group (USA) Inc.

First Printing, August 2008
10 9 8 7 6 5 4 3 2 1

The first chapter of this book previously appeared in *Flathead Fury*, the three
hundred twenty-first volume in this series.

Copyright © Penguin Group (USA) Inc., 2008
All rights reserved

 REGISTERED TRADEMARK—MARCA REGISTRADA

Printed in the United States of America

PUBLISHER'S NOTE
This is a work of fiction. Names, characters, places, and incidents either are the product of the author's imagination or are used fictitiously, and any resemblance to actual persons, living or dead, events, or locales is entirely coincidental.

The publisher does not have any control over and does not assume any responsibility for author or third-party Web sites or their content.

The Trailsman

Beginnings . . . they bend the tree and they mark the man. Skye Fargo was born when he was eighteen. Terror was his midwife, vengeance his first cry. Killing spawned Skye Fargo, ruthless, cold-blooded murder. Out of the acrid smoke of gunpowder still hanging in the air, he rose, cried out a promise never forgotten.

The Trailsman they began to call him all across the West: searcher, scout, hunter, the man who could see where others only looked, his skills for hire but not his soul, the man who lived each day to the fullest, yet trailed each tomorrow. Skye Fargo, the Trailsman, the seeker who could take the wildness of a land and the wanting of a woman and make them his own.

The Territory of New Mexico, 1861—
a hotbed of hate and greed.

1

Skye Fargo had a bad feeling about the place.

It was named Hot Springs. It was not much of anything except a few cabins and shacks and the inevitable saloon. Then there was the structure built over the hot springs, which reminded him of a Navajo hogan, only it was the size of a small hill.

Fargo wanted a drink and a meal he did not cook himself so he rode down the short dusty street to the hitch rail in front of the saloon and stiffly dismounted. He had been in the saddle since daybreak, and here it was almost sundown.

Tall and broad of shoulder, Fargo wore buckskins, a hat that had once been white but was now dust brown, and a red bandanna. Women were fond of his ruggedly handsome face. Men who had heard of him were wary of his fists and his Colt. Stretching, he sauntered into the saloon. After the harsh glare of the sun it took a few seconds for his eyes to adjust to the gloom. He paid no attention to the customers at the tables but walked right to the bar, smacked it loud enough to get the bartender to start in his direction, and demanded, "Whiskey."

If there was anything better for soothing a dry throat, Fargo had yet to find it. He drained his first glass at a gulp and motioned for more, then decided to hell with it and paid for the bottle. Taking it to a corner table, he sank down with a sigh and prepared to get pleasantly soused. He frowned when two pairs of boots came toward his table, and looked up to see who filled them.

The one on the right was short and thin and had eyes an owl would envy. He was dressed in a costly store-bought suit and his boots had been polished to a fine shine.

The one on the left was muscle, and a lot of it. Over six feet and over two hundred and fifty pounds, if Fargo was any judge. This one wore a well-used shirt and pants, and his boots were scuffed. The scars on his knuckles gave warning his hands were not ornaments.

"Go away," Fargo said.

Both men stopped and the owl blinked in surprise. "You have not heard what I have to say."

"I don't want to hear it." Fargo set him straight. "Go away."

"I am afraid I can't," the owl said. "I am Timothy P. Cranmeyer of the Cranmeyer Freight Company."

Fargo was amused. "You named your company after yourself?"

"A common enough practice," Cranmeyer said amiably. "But that is neither here nor there. We need to talk."

"No, we do not," Fargo said as he filled his glass.

"I cannot say I think much of your attitude. I am an important man in these parts."

Fargo snorted.

Cranmeyer colored, then jerked a thumb at the muscle next to him. "This is Mr. Krupp. He works for me. He is the captain of my freight train."

"Good for him," Fargo said, a bit testy now that the man would not take the hint.

The muscle spoke. "I make sure people show Mr. Cranmeyer the respect he deserves."

Fargo's hand came up from under the table, holding his Colt. He set it on the table with a loud *thunk*. "Here is your respect, Cranmeyer. Take your pet bear and go annoy someone else."

Amazingly, Timothy P. Cranmeyer did no such thing.

"You will hear me out whether you want to or not. It is in your own best interest."

Skye Fargo sighed. "If there is one thing this world does not have a shortage of, it is idiots."

"You look as if you can handle yourself in a scrap and I have need of men to help guard my freight wagons. They are bound for Silver Lode up in the Mimbres Mountains and will be here by noon tomorrow. I rode on ahead."

"Good for you," Fargo said, and drained half the glass. "I am not interested."

"I will pay you sixty dollars for two weeks' work," Cranmeyer persisted. "You must admit that is good money."

That it was, but Fargo had a full poke. "I am still not interested. I am on my way north, not west."

"The Fraziers are driving the wagons," Cranmeyer said, as if that should mean something.

"Mister, I do not care if the president, the pope, and the queen of England are driving. You are a nuisance. Skedaddle, and be quick about it. My patience has flown out the window."

Krupp's voice was as deep and low as a well. "Do you want me to teach him some respect, Mr. Cranmeyer?"

Fargo placed his hand on his Colt. "Be my guest. I have not shot anyone in a few days and am out of practice."

Showing no fear, Krupp balled his big fists. "Are you so yellow you can't do it without that?"

"There is an epidemic of stupid," Fargo said, and flicked his Colt up. At the blast, Krupp's hat did a somersault and flopped to the floor between the two men. Krupp stood there as calm as could be but Cranmeyer started and took a step back.

"You are awful quick on the trigger."

"Only when I am mad, and thanks to you I am mad as hell." Fargo pointed the Colt at him. "For the last time. Make yourself scarce or you will have to make do without an ear."

"I do not think much of your manners," Cranmeyer said stiffly.

"I don't give a good damn whether you do or you don't. I will count to ten and then the perforating begins." Fargo paused, then began his count. "Four. Five. Six. Sev—"

"Hold on. What happened to one, two and three?"

"They flew out the window with my patience." Fargo resumed his count. "Seven. Eight. Ni—"

"All right. All right." Cranmeyer held up both hands. "I am leaving. But if you change your mind, I will be in Hot Springs until about two tomorrow afternoon. That is when I hope to leave for Silver Lode."

Fargo did not hide his surprise. "You *still* want to hire me?"

"I told you. I need men who are not trigger-shy, and anyone who will shoot me over a trifle will more than likely not mind shooting Apaches and anyone else who might give me trouble."

Despite himself, Fargo laughed. "Look, Cranmeyer. I do not need the money. And I am not in the mood to tangle with the Mimbres Apaches. I have done it before and been lucky to get away with my hide."

"I thought so," Cranmeyer said, and smiled. "You look like a man who is more wolf than sheep."

"Save the flattery. I still won't go."

"Did I mention the Fraziers are driving three of the wagons? That is usually enough to entice most."

"Why in hell would I care who the drivers are? Mule skinners interest me about as much as head lice."

Now it was Cranmeyer who laughed. "I take it you have never heard of the Fraziers, then?"

"Should I?"

"Word has gotten around. You see, as mule skinners go they are special in that they are females. Sisters, no less, with a reputation for being as wild and reckless as can be."

Fargo was genuinely surprised. Mule skinning was hard, brutal, dangerous work. He had only ever met one

4

other woman who did it for a living, and she had the misfortune to be born a man in a woman's body. "I am still not interested." He was, however, curious.

"Very well. I tried." Disappointed, Cranmeyer turned. "Come along, Krupp. We will see if there is anyone else we might hire. I must replace the three who quit on me or we will not have enough protection when we start up into the mountains."

Krupp, scowling, picked up his hat.

Fargo could not resist asking, "Why did they quit on you?"

Cranmeyer looked back. "One of them tried to take liberties with Myrtle Frazier and she took a whip to him. It embarrassed him, being beaten by a woman. He quit, and his friends left with him."

"So you weren't kidding when you said these women are wildcats."

"Mister, you have no idea. If they weren't three of the best mule skinners in all of the Territory of New Mexico, I would have nothing to do with them. At times they can be almost more trouble than they are worth."

Fargo took a sip. He had not been with a woman in a while, and if there was one thing he could not do without, besides whiskey, it was women. He had half a mind to look up the Frazier sisters when the freight wagons arrived. But if Myrtle was any example, all he would get for his interest was the lash of her bullwhip. He shrugged and decided to forget them.

Before long the sun set and some of the citizens of Hot Springs, a paltry dozen or so, drifted into the saloon to indulge in their nightly ritual.

The bartender turned out to be the owner, and he turned out to have a wife who was also the cook. Fargo ordered a thick slab of steak with all the trimmings and a pot of coffee to wash the food down. He was halfway through the steak, chewing a delicious piece of fat, when a new arrival perked his interest. She was young and saucy and had curly red hair, and she sashayed into the saloon as if she had the best pair of legs a dress ever clung to. The locals grinned and greeted her warmly, and in return received pats on the back or the backside or in a few cases a peck on the cheek. She handed her shawl to the bartender, gazed about the room, blinked and came strolling over with her hands on her hips and an enticing grin on her lips.

"Well, what do we have here? You are new. Are you staying a spell or just passing through?"

"The only way I would stay more than one night is if I was six feet under," Fargo said.

"Hot Springs isn't *that* bad," the vixen replied, chortling. "But I will admit that there is not a whole lot to do around here except sit in the hot spring and sweat."

Fargo showed his teeth in a roguish smirk. "I can think of another way to work up a sweat, and it is a lot more fun than sitting in scalding-hot water."

She looked him up and down, and nodded. "I reckon you could, at that." Offering her hand, she said, "I am Tilly Jones. Do you have a handle or do I just call you Good-Looking?" She let the clasp linger and when she pulled her hand back, she slid her middle finger across his palm.

Fargo was interested. He needed something to do until dawn and she would do nicely. Quite nicely, in fact. "What time do you get done here?"

"My, oh, my." Tilly grinned. "You could at least introduce yourself. Or are you a randy goat who only thinks of one thing?"

"I am no goat," Fargo said. "But I still think of that one thing a lot." He introduced himself.

"Right pleased to make your acquaintance." Tilly pulled out a chair. "How about if you buy me a drink or I will have to go to talk to someone else. Sam over yonder isn't happy unless I am making him money."

A wave of Fargo's arm brought the bartender with an extra glass. Fargo filled it and watched with admiration as she swallowed half. "You have had red-eye before."

Laughing, Tilly smacked her delightfully full strawberry lips. "More times than either of us can count. I daresay I can drink most any man here under the table."

"You are welcome to try," Fargo challenged.

Swirling the whiskey in her glass, Tilly replied, "Don't think I wouldn't. But if we are to have a frolic later, I best stay sober." She glanced at the batwings, worry in her emerald eyes, and bit her lower lip.

"Something wrong?"

"Oh, nothing I can't take care of. This gent strayed in about a week ago and took a shine to me, and the next thing I knew he was following me around like a little calf, making cow eyes and saying as how the two of us were meant for each other."

Fargo chuckled. Some people equated passion with love. A silly notion, but then a hunger for a female had made many a man do damned silly things.

"It is not all that humorous," Tilly said. "He has gone from being an amusement to a bother I can do without." Suddenly she stiffened and her hand rose to her throat.

The batwings had parted and in marched a rail-thin apparition with a bushy beard, a tangle of black hair and a nose like a hawk's beak. His dirty clothes and the pick wedged under his belt marked him as a prospector. He had to be in his middle twenties. He spotted Tilly and strode over, shoving aside two men who were in his way.

"Here you are."

"Go away, Stein. I am working."

Ignoring Fargo, Stein gripped her arm and tried to pull her to her feet but she resisted. "I don't care what you are doing. You have put me off long enough. I am taking you back up into the mountains with me."

"Like hell you are," Tilly said.

"I will not take no for an answer." Stein tugged on her again with the same result. "The sooner you get it through your pretty head that from now on you are mine and only mine, the better off you will be."

"Leave me alone!" Tilly snapped. "Or I will go to the law and file a complaint."

"What law?" Stein scoffed. "The nearest tin star is hundreds of miles away." He gripped her chin. "On your feet."

Fargo had witnessed enough. Sliding his chair back, he came around the table and put his hand on Stein's shoulder. "The lady doesn't want your company. Light a shuck while you still can."

Stein straightened and pushed Fargo's hand off. "I don't take kindly to meddlers, and I take even less kindly to being told what to do." He slid the pick from under his belt. "You are the one who will make himself scarce, or by the eternal I will cave in your damn skull."

2

There were things Skye Fargo could not abide. Being threatened was one. Being pushed was another. Being told what to do was a third. The man called Stein had managed to do all three.

Another thing Fargo did not much care for was mistreating women and horses. A good horse, in his opinion, was more than an animal; it was a friend. To see a horse abused always rankled him. As for women, he was no knight in shining armor, but when one was being treated as Tilly was being treated, it made him want to stomp the prospector into the ground, preferably with a few teeth kicked in. So Fargo had plenty of motivation to do what he did next—namely, launch his fist from his hip and catch Stein flush on the jaw. For most that was enough. Fargo was big and he was rawhide tough. One punch would lay a man out as cold as ice.

But Stein had an iron jaw. Hitting it was like hitting an anvil. Stein staggered against another table and had to brace himself against it to stay on his feet, but he did not go down. Instead, shaking his head to clear it, he hefted his pick and straightened.

"Mister, you just bought yourself a whole heap of trouble."

Fargo could have drawn his Colt and shot him. But he was not a cold-blooded killer. He had never crossed that line, and saw no need to cross it now. Not when he had the reflexes of a mountain lion and the brawn of a bear. "Get the hell out of here."

With a snarl of fury, Stein attacked. Whipping the pick over his head, he drove it at Fargo's forehead. He was fast, too, faster than Fargo reckoned, and it was all Fargo could do to twist aside in time so that the pick swept past his face and thudded into the table within a few inches of Tilly, causing her to cry out.

In lightning blows, Fargo caught Stein in the stomach and again on the jaw. Stein tottered, but as before, he recovered with uncanny quickness, set himself and came at Fargo again.

"I will kill you, you bastard!"

Blowhards were another of Fargo's peeves. Maybe it stemmed from the fact he was not all that talkative by nature, and tended to say what he needed to say in as few words as possible. One thing he never, ever, did was indulge in idle threats. When he needed to hurt someone, he did it and that was that. He did not boast about what he was going to do beforehand.

He needed to hurt Stein before that pick hurt him. Accordingly, when Stein slashed at his chest, Fargo side-stepped, caught hold of Stein's arm and drove his knee into the prospector's elbow.

Stein shrieked. He almost dropped the pick. Tearing loose, he stepped back and doubled over, his arm pressed to his belly.

"Had enough?" Fargo asked.

The man had the common sense of a turnip. Roaring with rage, he switched the pick to his other hand and came at Fargo again.

Fargo evaded two swift swings. He landed a jab to the ribs that made Stein flinch and recoil, and then he delivered an uppercut that started down near the floor. This time Stein was rocked onto his heels and teetered like a tree about to be uprooted. Swooping his hand to his Colt, Fargo streaked it up and out and slammed the barrel against Stein's temple.

The prospector folded without a sound and lay in a heap, twitching.

Tilly had risen and was standing with her back to the wall, her eyes wide, her hand to her throat. "Oh, my."

"Something wrong?" Fargo asked as he twirled the Colt into its holster.

"You were magnificent!"

Fargo bent and picked up the pick. The bartender was coming over and he tossed it to him, saying, "Hide this. Give it back the next time he is in here." Then, gripping Stein by the collar, he dragged the unconscious lump from the saloon. The place was quiet enough to hear a pin drop. All eyes were on him; no one objected or interfered. He left Stein lying by the hitch rail and went back in.

Tilly had reclaimed her seat and was tilting his whiskey bottle to her lips. She chugged like a cavalry trooper and did not cough when she set the bottle down. "I hope you don't mind me helping myself."

"I am just glad you saved some for me," Fargo said, taking the bottle from her as he dropped into his chair.

"You sure know how to take care of yourself. He never so much as scratched you."

"I was lucky."

"You are good," Tilly said. "It serves him right for being a jackass. If it had been me, I'd have hit him a few more times with that pistol. Maybe bust his nose or break a few teeth."

"You are a bloodthirsty wench," Fargo remarked with a smile.

"Not really. I am just tired of men who think God gave them the right to paw every woman they meet. I don't mind a pat on the fanny now and then, but the pinches and groping I can do without." Tilly fluffed her hair. "Now then. Enough about lunkheads like Stein. I want to know all there is to know about a gent named Skye Fargo."

"I would like to go to bed with you."

Tilly blinked and sat back in surprise, then snickered. "Are you always so blunt?"

"I have been without a woman for a week. I want to strip off that dress and run my hands over every square inch of your body. I want to do some of that pinching and groping you don't like until you are fit to explode."

Smiling sheepishly, Tilly said, "With the right gent, I *do* like it. But I must say, you do not beat around the bush."

"The only bush here is yours, and there are better things to do with it," Fargo said.

Tilly's mouth dropped and for a few seconds she was speechless. Then she burst into hearty mirth. "My word! You make a girl warm all over, the way you talk."

"I have not even begun to warm you up," Fargo teased.

Leaning on her elbows, Tilly said softly, "I love a man with a sense of humor. Dullards can make even that *that* boring."

"Take me home with you and we will have a night that is anything but dull," Fargo said.

"I love a man with confidence, too," Tilly bantered, and reaching across, she squeezed his hand. "Mister, you have a date. As soon as I am off, you are mine to do with as I please."

The promise in her tone hinted that Fargo was in for a night he would not soon forget. He settled back to finish his meal while she mingled. The food was cold but he didn't mind. He chewed lustily and washed it down with whiskey.

The saloon returned to normal. The buzz of talk blended with the clink of poker chips and the tinkle of glass. Oaths and guffaws punctuated the general good cheer. Cigar and pipe smoke rose to the rafters. Tilly roved freely, encouraging customers to drink and gamble and have a good time.

Fargo was feeling pretty good himself when, along about ten o'clock, he stepped outside to check on the Ovaro and to get some fresh air. Stein was gone. Good riddance, Fargo thought, and turned toward the water trough. Just then a rifle boomed and the slug meant to core his head struck the saloon with a loud *thwack*. Fargo dived flat. Clawing at his Colt, he rolled toward the far end of the trough.

People in the saloon were yelling. From a shack next door stepped an old man who demanded to know what the shooting was about.

Shoving onto his knees, Fargo scanned the other side of the street. Except for rectangles of light spilling from windows, the night was black as pitch. The shooter could be anywhere, waiting for a clear shot.

Fargo could not stay behind the trough. Not when one of the horses might take a stray slug. Heaving upright, he ran toward the corner of the saloon and made it just as the rifle boomed again. This time he glimpsed the muzzle flash. Whirling, he answered with two swift shots and was rewarded with a yelp of pain or surprise. Darting around the corner, he hurriedly replaced the spent cartridges.

Hot Springs was as quiet as a tomb save for the mewing of a cat. Not so much as a peep came from the saloon, and the old man had ducked back inside his shack. The populace was holding its collective breath, awaiting the outcome.

Fargo knew who was out to plant him. Cupping a hand to his mouth, he hollered, "You don't handle a rifle any better than you do that pick of yours!"

Stein's mocking laugh came from the vicinity of a stand of saplings near a cabin. "I would have blown a hole in your skull if you hadn't turned your damn head when I squeezed the trigger!"

"If you are smart, you will leave Hot Springs." Not that Fargo gave a damn. But he could do without the nuisance of having to kill the man.

"You don't fool me. You want me to go because you are scared. You aren't so tough when you're not pistol-whipping someone."

"Jackass."

More laughter from the stand. "You buckskin boys are

13

all the same. You act like you own the world. Soon there will be one less of your breed, and that one less will be you. Do you hear me?"

Fargo did, but he was running toward the rear of the saloon and couldn't answer. He flew around the corner and kept on past more shacks and a tent. The interior was lit, and the silhouette of a woman moved across the canvas. Fargo was so intent on the silhouette that he forgot about Stein and paid for his neglect when lead nearly took off his head. Hunkering, he figured there would be another shot and a muzzle flash to shoot at but Stein was being cagey.

"Is somebody out there?" the woman in the tent called out.

"No," Fargo said, and ran on. His intent was to circle around to the other side of the street. The last building on his side was the hoganlike structure that enclosed the hot springs. It was closed and dark. Over two stories high, the dome reared above him as he crept along with his back to the wall. He was halfway around when the *crunch* of a footstep warned him someone was coming from the other direction.

It had to be Stein, Fargo reckoned. They both had the same idea. If he stood perfectly still, the prospector would walk right into his sights. Holding his breath, he waited, but the footfalls had stopped.

Stein must have heard *him*.

Now it was cat and mouse, and Fargo never could stand being the mouse. In a crouch he inched forward, his Colt extended. Stein, he expected, was doing the same. At any instant a darkling shape would appear and he would put two or three slugs into it.

Fargo's skin prickled. He was primed to fire but there was no one to shoot. Stein did not appear. No one did. Fargo went two-thirds of the way along the building, and nothing. Puzzled, he stopped and strained his ears but all he heard was the wind.

Could he have been mistaken? Fargo asked himself. No, he was certain he heard a footstep. If he was right, and it had been Stein, then the prospector had retraced his steps and could be anywhere, lying in ambush. In which case, Fargo felt it best to flatten and crawl. He came to the far side and still no Stein. His puzzlement growing, he rose and cat-footed toward the saplings. He doubted Stein was there, and it would be good cover.

The street was empty except for the horses at the hitch rail. Someone was at the batwings but did not come out.

The trees were mired in inky shadow. Fargo threaded along the outer edge until he reached a vantage point that gave him a clear view of the street and the buildings on both sides.

Where in hell could the prospector have gotten to? Fargo wondered, and had his question answered by furtive movement near the horses. Stein was near where he had been minutes ago; they had changed places. He raised his Colt but could not see well enough to shoot.

Anger bubbled inside him. All he had wanted was some food, some bug juice, and some rest. And now look. But then, that was one of the things he liked best about the frontier. A man never knew but that he would happen on hostiles in war paint or be confronted by a hungry griz or fall from his horse and break a leg. Life was unpredictable, and he liked it that way. He could never live in a town, where each day was a repeat of the day before, where people lived in cages made not of bars but of their own habits.

The crack of a twig brought Fargo out of himself. Something, or someone, was in the stand with him. He glanced at the horse trough but did not see anyone. It occurred to him that maybe he had been mistaken, that Stein was not over near the saloon but was right there in the trees.

His nerves on edge, Fargo slowly shifted. He held the Colt low against his leg so the metal would not glint and give him away. The sound had come from off to his right. He peered intently into the gloom but nothing moved. Neither did he. If he had to, he could stay motionless for hours; he would wait the bastard out.

Then a shape acquired form and substance, slinking warily toward him. Inwardly Fargo smiled as he curled his finger around the Colt's trigger. He was a heartbeat from firing when the last thing he expected to happen, happened.

"Skye? Is that you?" Tilly Jones whispered.

Fargo was dumbfounded. He had assumed she was safe in the saloon. Acutely conscious that Stein might be lurking close by, he darted over, seized her wrist and yanked her none too gently down beside him. "What the hell are you doing here?"

Tilly drew back in alarm. "Why are you so mad? I heard the shooting and came looking for you."

"Of all the damn fool stunts," Fargo growled, probing the night around them.

"Is this the thanks I get for being worried?"

"It is the thanks you get for not staying put as you should have," Fargo gruffly responded.

"I thought I saw someone over here and figured it might be you," Tilly explained, plainly hurt.

"And now what? Do I take you back to the saloon and maybe be shot crossing the street?" Fargo was being hard on her but she deserved it. She had not thought it out.

"I honestly don't see why you are so upset."

Fargo was about to enlighten her when a hard object was jammed against his spine and a gun hammer clicked.

"I know why," Stein said. "And I want to thank you, Tilly, for making it so easy."

3

Fargo wanted to beat his head against one of the trees. He had been so intent on Tilly he had let down his guard. He braced for the shot but none came. Instead, the rifle gouged harder into his spine.

"This is how we will do this," Stein said. "You will hand your pistol to me over your left shoulder. Any tricks, any twitches, and I squeeze this trigger and blow you to hell."

"Stein, listen—" Tilly began.

"Shut your mouth," the prospector snapped. "You will not talk unless I say to, or I will shoot him. If you move, I will shoot him. Do anything at all to make me mad, and I will shoot the bastard."

Tilly opened her mouth but closed it again.

"Good girl." Stein mocked her. He jabbed his rifle into Fargo again. "Now the pistol. Nice and slow, mister."

Fargo had no choice. He could whirl and try to wrest the rifle away, or he could spring to one side, but in either case he might take a slug. He slid the Colt over his left shoulder and it was snatched from his fingers.

Stein's laugh was ice and menace. "Well, now. This makes things simpler." The pressure of the muzzle eased and he came around in front of them, his rifle trained on Fargo, his teeth showing in the dark. "I should shoot you here and now but I won't. Care to guess why?"

Fargo did not need to guess. He had met men like this prospector before. "You want to hear yourself talk."

Stein's smirk became a scowl. "I would watch what I say, were I you. You beat on me. You threw me out in the street. I owe you, mister, for the pain and the humiliation."

Tilly chimed in with, "You brought that on yourself. I kept telling you to leave me be, George."

"Now you are calling me by my first name?" Stein said. "Why so friendly all of a sudden? Could it be you hope to melt me with charm so I will let your new friend live?"

"Please," Tilly said.

"Please what?" Suddenly Stein bent toward them, his features those of a mad beast. "How stupid do you think I am, bitch? You had your chance. I courted you proper and you threw it in my face."

"Since when is trying to force a woman to go with a man against her will *courting*?" Tilly angrily demanded.

"I don't see what you are complaining about. I didn't hit you or anything, did I?"

Tilly started to rise but caught herself. "Is that your notion of love? You treat a woman like she is your slave and you are her master, but you don't hit her, so that makes it right?"

"Who said anything about love?" Stein retorted. "I just want a warm body on cold nights. I want someone to do the cooking and washing and sweep the floor now and again."

"I was right. You do want a slave."

Stein took a half step toward her. "I want a *woman*! You have no idea how lonely it can be up in those mountains. Night after night with just you and your thoughts to keep you company."

"There is Silver Lode," Tilly said.

"That shows how much you know. Silver Lode is a bunch of tents and drunks, and no women. No women will go up there because of the Apaches. They are too afraid."

"I don't blame them," Tilly said.

"I do. I cannot do without," Stein flatly declared. "I want one and I will have one, and that one is you."

"Why am I so lucky?"

Stein shrugged. "You are the first female I set eyes on when I got here. Besides, you are a dove. You make your living pleasing men. You don't have a husband or kids or any of that baggage. So I am taking you back up into the mountains with me."

"You are despicable," Tilly said. "If I had a knife, I would stab you."

Fargo had a knife. An Arkansas toothpick, which he wore in an ankle sheath. While they argued he had slid his hand under his pant leg and was inching his fingers into his boot.

"It won't be so bad," Stein was saying. "I will treat you decent. I won't beat you unless you deserve it, and I have a washtub so you can take baths like women like to do."

"I would live like a queen."

"Don't be that way. I may not have much now but when I do you will share in my wealth."

"You will give me half?" Tilly asked, her tone suggesting she was being sarcastic again.

"I won't go that far, no. But I will give you what is fair for the time you spend with me. Say, a hundred dollars a month. But only if I strike it rich. If I don't, I will give you what I can."

"And I have no say in any of this," Tilly said bitterly. "What do you think women are? Dogs in dresses?"

Fargo gripped the toothpick's hilt. But he did not use it. Not yet. Not until he was good and sure.

"You say the strangest things," Stein told Tilly. "Dogs don't wear clothes and women don't trot around on all fours."

"We might as well. Men like you don't treat us any better than they do their mongrels." Tilly sadly shook her head. "All my life I have had to deal with your kind. All my life I have hated them. Give me a man who treats a gal with respect. Give me a man who treats a woman like a woman and not like a cur."

"You are making a heap out of nothing," Stein criticized. "Get used to the idea that you are mine. As soon as I deal with him"—he jerked a thumb at Fargo—"you and me are heading for the high country."

"I will be damned if I am."

"You will be dead if you don't."

Tilly showed the whites of her eyes. "You would really do that? Kill me for not wanting to share your bed?"

"I am desperate for a female," Stein said. "I would not have come all the way down here if I wasn't."

"Why not pay for a poke and get it out of your system? I do not do pokes for money but Bucktoothed Mary does. She lives in the third shack past the saloon."

"A single poke will not do me," Stein said. "I want it every night that I am in the mood, and I am in the mood a lot."

"Of course you are. You are male." Tilly considered a bit, then said, "I will go with you willingly on one condition."

Stein was as surprised as Fargo by her abrupt change of heart. "How's that again?"

Tilly pointed at Fargo. "Let him live and I will go up into the mountains with you."

"Why so generous all of a sudden?" Stein suspiciously asked. "And why do you care so much about this saddle bum? What is he to you?"

"I never set eyes on him before tonight," Tilly confessed.

Stein sniffed as if he smelled a foul odor. "I was not born yesterday. No woman does what you are doing for a complete stranger. I repeat. What makes him so damn special?"

"He is something you can never be."

"And what would that be?"

Tilly did not reply.

"I asked you a question," Stein growled, taking another half step. He raised the rifle as if to bash her across the face with the stock. "Answer me, damn you, and answer me now."

"It is simple," Tilly said. "He knows how to treat a lady and you do not." She paused. "He is not scum and you are."

Cursing viciously and lunging at her, Stein hiked his rifle higher. "That is the last time you will belittle me."

Fargo had been hoping he would come closer; now he was within arm's reach. "I reckon it is only fair."

Stein glanced at him in confusion. "What is?"

"You snuck up behind me when I was arguing with her, and now you are arguing with her and I have had the time I need."

"Time for what?" Stein demanded.

"For this," Fargo said, and surged out of his crouch with his knife arm spearing up and around in an arc that ended with the double-edged blade buried to the hilt in Stein's chest.

George Stein bleated like a stricken ram and staggered back. The toothpick came out, and with it a scarlet torrent. He made no attempt to level his rifle, but stumbled against a tree. "What have you done to me?"

"What have *you* done?" Fargo amended. He felt no sympathy. The fool had brought it down on his own head.

The rifle clattered at Stein's feet. He placed a hand to his wound and drew it away dark with blood. "Oh, God." Turning toward Tilly, he held out his dripping hand. "All I wanted was some company."

"You will have plenty of company in hell," Fargo said, and stabbed him again, in the heart.

Stein threw back his head and gasped. He tried to speak but all that came out was blood. He started to quake and fell to his knees. Clutching wildly at thin air, he gurgled. Froth dribbled from his mouth. It was the last sound he uttered. Going as rigid as a ramrod, he pitched onto his face, convulsed and was still.

"That was ugly," Tilly said.

"It was him or me and I was damned if it was going

to be me." Fargo wiped the toothpick clean on Stein's shirt and replaced it in his ankle sheath. Reclaiming his Colt, he shoved it into its holster. "Let's go," he said, offering his arm.

"What about the body?"

"Is there an undertaker in Hot Springs?"

"If there is, he is keeping himself well hid. The town is not big enough. Give us four or five years."

Fargo had half a mind to treat the coyotes and other scavengers to a feast. But he had seen a few children earlier. It would not do to have them come across a rotting body. "Is there someone who will bury your late admirer for, say, a dollar?" That was all he was willing to pay.

"I bet I can find you someone for half that," Tilly said. "Money is hard to come by in these parts. There are not many jobs to be had."

Hot Springs was unnaturally quiet, the street still empty. Heads were poking out the saloon door, and when Fargo and Tilly appeared, shouts broke out and men came streaming through the batwings.

The prospector's death was the most exciting thing to happen in Hot Springs in a coon's age. Most of the hamlet's populace came out to view the body and to tell what they were doing when the shots rang out. A few bragged that they heard Stein's death rattle. One man even claimed to have witnessed the stabbing, but since he lived at the other end of the street and was toting a half-empty bottle of red-eye, no one believed him.

Fargo wanted nothing to do with the shenanigans. He roosted in his chair at the corner table in the saloon and renewed his assault on his own bottle. He had never been one of those who took delight in viewing violence or its aftermath. When he came on a wrecked wagon or an overturned buckboard, he was not the kind to stand and gawk. Spilled blood did not hold the warped fascination for him that it held for so many.

Fargo had seen too much blood spilling to regard it as entertainment. Life on the frontier was savage and hard, especially for those who dared venture into country few whites if any had ever set foot in. The mountains and prairies were the killing grounds for hostiles and renegades who had no qualms about murdering every innocent they came across.

The tally of wounded or dead Fargo had come across, or helped send to the other side, would fill a city the size of Santa Fe. To him the violence was as much a part of the frontier as the mountains and the prairies themselves.

Fargo had the saloon to himself. Even the man who owned it and his wife had gone to see the body. Tilly was off finding someone to do the burying. He was on his third chug, the bottle upended over his mouth, when the batwings parted and in came the last two people he wanted to see. Smacking the bottle down, he said gruffly, "Go away."

"We have as much right to be here are you do," Timothy P. Cranmeyer said. "Saloons are open to the public, after all."

"Just so you are not here to badger me," Fargo warned.

"As a matter of fact," Cranmeyer said, "I would like to make the same offer I made earlier. Come work for me for two weeks and I will pay you seventy-five dollars."

"Earlier it was sixty."

"Earlier I only had a hunch you are the kind of man I need," Cranmeyer said. "Now I am sure of it. You are not squeamish about killing."

"Only when I have to."

"Frankly, I don't care why you do it just so you will squeeze the trigger if we are set upon by Apaches or others. A lot of men lose their heads and their nerves and can't or won't."

Fargo had sometimes wondered how it was that some men could not kill, no matter what. "No."

"What will it take to persuade you?"

Fargo sighed. "Let me make it plain. There is no chance in hell. Not now. Not tomorrow. Not ever. Run

23

along or I will throw you out like I did that other idiot lying over in the trees."

"Honestly, now," Cranmeyer said.

"Jackass."

Krupp chose that moment to start around the table, declaring, "That does it. I warned you about insulting Mr. Cranmeyer. The only way to teach you some respect is to pound it into you."

4

It was Fargo's night for lunkheads. He pushed out of his chair, his fists balled. In the mood he was in, he was the one who would do the pounding.

But before the slab of muscle could reach him, Cranmeyer hastily intervened. "There will be none of that, Mr. Krupp. I came in here to talk. Nothing more."

Krupp stopped but he was not pleased. "You heard how he talks to you. I can't allow that."

"Again, I decide what I will and will not allow," Cranmeyer said curtly. "You will do as I say or you will seek employment elsewhere."

Sullenly glaring at Fargo, Krupp relented. "This is not over, mister. Something tells me that sooner or later you and me are going to bump heads, and when we do, you are the one who will be shy some teeth."

"Anytime you want to bleed, look me up," Fargo countered.

"I swear," Cranmeyer said. "You two are worse than twelve-year-olds. But there are better ways to settle disputes than with violence."

Just then the batwings creaked and in came Tilly Jones, her shawl over her shoulders. She looked flustered and said with a sharp gesture, "I swear! If people were any more stupid, they would not have any brains at all."

"Is something the matter, Miss Jones?" Cranmeyer asked.

"Only that they expect me to stand out there and tell

them every little detail about what led up to the killing. I started to explain that Stein had been hounding me for some time to go up into the mountains with him, and one fool had the gall to ask if I ever slept with him!" Tilly swore. "As if I ever would. But the point is that my personal life is my own, and they can all go to hell." She came to the corner table, placed her hand on Fargo's shoulder and kissed him warmly on the cheek. "Did you miss me, handsome?"

For some reason, Timothy P. Cranmeyer lit up like a candle and said cheerfully, "So it was jealously that spawned the fight."

"Weren't you listening?" Tilly said harshly. "My personal life is my own. If I happen to find a man attractive, that is my business and no one else's."

"My dear, I could not agree more," Cranmeyer said. "And I am delighted that your new friend here is fond enough of you to kill a man in your defense."

Fargo was puzzled by the remark, and so, apparently, was Tilly.

"Why is that?"

"It means he is fond of women."

"Most men are," Tilly wryly observed. "If they weren't, the human race would not be around long."

Cranmeyer chuckled, then touched his hat brim to her and nodded at Fargo. "This has been illuminating. We will talk again, sir." Wheeling on a heel, he crooked a finger at Krupp and they departed.

"What in God's name was that all about?" Tilly wondered aloud.

"I wish I knew." Fargo had a hunch that Cranmeyer was up to something, but what it could be was beyond him. He shrugged it away, saying, "Let's forget about him and forget about Stein and start thinking about you and me."

"You and me how?" Tilly asked with an impish grin.

Looping an arm around her slender waist, Fargo pulled her down onto his lap. "Guess," he said, and molded his mouth to her warm lips. Hers parted, and her tongue entwined with his. She could kiss, this gal. When they broke for air, both of them were flushed.

"Oh, my. That was nice."

"There is more where that came from," Fargo said.

"I don't get off until midnight," Tilly informed him. "If you want, you can wait for me at my place. I have a small shack all to myself at the west end of the street. Do you want the key?"

Fargo had intended to play some poker but it appeared that it would be a while before the excitement outside died and the saloon refilled. And, too, he had been on the trail so long, he could stand to wash up and trim his beard. "Don't mind if I do."

"Pay no mind to Cyclops if he is there. I keep a window cracked for him and he comes and goes pretty much as he pleases."

"Cyclops?" Fargo repeated.

"My cat. Or maybe I am his. He showed up on my doorstep one day. I gave him some milk, and the next thing I knew, he had moved in." Tilly laughed. "I have always liked cats more than dogs. How about you?"

Fargo could do without either. Dogs slobbered and chewed shoes and sniffed other dogs' hind ends. Cats scratched up everything and coughed up hairballs and only let themselves be petted when they wanted to be petted. Give him a good horse over a dog or cat any day. Horses did not whine and bark. Horses did not shed hair all over and have litters with ten more of their kind. "I am partial to lizards," he joked.

"Let me fetch my key. It is in my bag behind the bar."

Her shack did not have much to distinguish it beyond frilly drapes in the window and a row of flowers under it. Fargo let himself in. He turned to the left, groping for a small table with a lamp that was supposed to be there. His right boot came down on something that felt like a rope, and the next instant an ear-splitting shriek filled the shack and a furry form hurtled past him and out the door.

"Stupid cat," Fargo grumbled. He had not meant to

step on its tail but if it rid him of the feline, so much the better.

The lamp was where Tilly had said it would be. Its rosy glow revealed a comfortably furnished room. In one corner was the bed, neatly made. In another was an oak dresser. In yet another, a stove. An oval rug with Oriental overtones covered the middle of the floor. The rug had seen a lot of wear, suggesting she had owned it a while.

Tilly did not have a lot of clothes; two dresses and a bonnet were in the closet. That was it. A cupboard contained dishes and pots and a frying pan. On a counter were a wash basin and a pitcher full of water.

With a grunt of satisfaction, Fargo placed his hat on the table. He stripped off his buckskin shirt and draped it over the chair. His gun belt, he put on the bed. Taking a towel from a hook on the wall and a washcloth from a bottom drawer of the dresser, he was about to begin when he realized that he had left his razor in his saddlebags, and his saddlebags were on the Ovaro.

Fargo went to the door. He had tied the stallion to a post out front. Once he was done washing, he would strip off the saddle and saddle blanket and catch forty winks before Tilly showed up. He opened the door, and froze.

The man who stood there practically filled the doorway. He was big, and so was the Walker Colt he held, already cocked. To say his clothes were filthy was being charitable. His mouth split in surprise, exposing yellow teeth, and he blurted, "How did you know I was out here, mister?"

Fargo did not like having revolvers pointed at him. Especially cocked revolvers. "Who the blazes are you?"

"You are the one who killed Stein."

"Oh, hell."

"You and me have issues," the man said, and wagged the Walker Colt. "Keep your hands where I can see them and back up until I tell you to stop."

Fargo was almost to the opposite wall before the man barked at him. He glanced at the bed, and his gun belt.

"Try for it and I will put holes in you."

"Do you have a name?"

"No. My ma and pa plumb forgot to give me one." The man thought he was hilarious, and laughed.

"How about if I call you Whiskey Breath?" Fargo said. The man reeked of booze and his eyes were bloodshot.

"If you are hankering to die you are going about it the right way." Whiskey Breath extended the revolver.

"You are here to kill me anyway." Fargo refused to stand there helpless and let it happen. There had to be something he could do.

"You should not go jumping to conclusions. Maybe I won't have to." Whiskey Breath entered and closed the door behind him. "I never said anything about blowing out your wick. I am here to talk. This hogleg is to make sure you don't do to me like you did to Stein."

Fargo suspected there was more to it but he did not say anything.

"But if you want me to shoot you, I will." The man tittered and swayed. He trained the Walker Colt on Fargo's legs. "Which one can you do without? I will be fair and let you decide."

"You're loco," Fargo said. And very, very drunk.

"If you won't pick one, I will." Whiskey Breath pointed the Walker at Fargo's right leg and then at the left and then at the right again. "Decisions, decisions."

Fargo tensed to dive for the bed and his Colt. He might take a slug but he would get off a few shots of his own.

"The shin or the knee? Which should it be?" Whiskey Breath chortled. "I would pick the shin but that is just me."

"Is this a game you are playing?"

"Hell, no," Whiskey Breath said. "This is serious as can be. I have as much right to it as anyone and more right than you."

"You have lost me," Fargo admitted.

"Stein has a claim close to mine up near Silver Lode. Or had, until you killed him. But where he took out silver now and again, my claim has hardly been worth the effort I have put into it. Not unless dirt is worth something these days." He chortled some more.

"What does any of that have to do with me?"

"The word on the street is that you and him fought over a female. But I figure the real reason is that you are a claim jumper and you want his claim for your own. It happens all the time."

"You really *are* loco."

Whiskey Breath ignored the remark. "With Stein dead, anyone can take over his claim. And that anyone is going to be me. I want it and I will have it, and you will agree or I will shoot you."

"So that is what this is about." Fargo smothered an urge to swear a mean streak. "Do I look like an ore hound to you? I have better things to do with my life than waste it grubbing in the ground."

"That is my livelihood you are insulting." Whiskey Breath displayed more of his yellow teeth. "Do we have an accord? Is Stein's claim mine?"

"Help yourself."

"Do you mean it? I don't want you back-shooting me later."

"Mister, I don't give a damn about it. I am on my way north and only passing through."

Whiskey Breath smiled and started to back toward the door. "This has turned out better than I reckoned. I will be on my way. You stand there and pretend you are a tree. Don't open this door for at least five minutes. By then I will be clear out of Hot Springs."

"You are heading up into the mountains at night?"

"Why not? It is safer than during the day. The Apaches can't spot me from a ways off. And anyway, folks say they don't attack much at night." Whiskey Breath reached behind him and felt for the latch. "I hope you will be sensible and not hold this against me."

"Quit jabbering and go." Fargo was tired of being imposed on. He just wanted the greedy bastard out of there.

That was when the door swung in, catching Whiskey Breath across the knuckles and eliciting a yelp of surprise and pain.

"Skye! I got off early—!" Tilly Jones caught herself and stepped back in alarm. "What in the world! What are you doing here, Tibbett? And why is your gun out?"

Apparently they knew one another. Fargo figured the foul-breathed prospector would make up some excuse and get out of there, but Tibbett grabbed Tilly by the wrist and practically flung her across the room, saying, "Damn it, woman! You would have to come back now!"

Tilly stumbled and would have fallen if Fargo had not caught her. "What is going on here?" she demanded. "Why is he holding a revolver on you?"

Before Fargo could explain, Tibbett slammed the door and whirled on them. He was literally twitching with anger. "This won't do. If it was just him it would be his word against mine. But now it is the two of you."

"What are you talking about?" Tilly asked.

"You are well liked," Tibbett said, more to himself than to her. "People are likely to take exception to me barging in here."

"People, hell," Tilly said. "*I* take exception. This might not be much of a home but it is mine and I will be damned if you or anyone else can march in here and wave a revolver around."

Fargo cut in before she made the situation worse. "Maybe you should give him your word you won't tell anyone and he will be on his way."

Tilly wasn't listening to him. "You haven't said what you are doing here, Tibbett. You better have a good excuse. The other prospectors won't take kindly to you treating me this way, females in these parts being so scarce and all."

"Promise him," Fargo urged.

But Tilly was mad and growing madder. "Cat got your

tongue? Why are you standing there with that pained look?"

Tibbett looked at his big Colt and then at them. "I didn't give it much thought before but I reckon I shouldn't let you or your friend go around telling what I did." He sadly shook his head. "I did not want to do this. You have brought it on yourself."

In sudden panic Tilly clutched at Fargo. "Will one of you *please* tell me what is going on?"

Tibbett came toward them, tilting like a sailor on a wave-tossed ship. "I am sorry. But I can't let word of this get out. I will make it quick so you don't suffer much."

Fargo inched toward the bed. Tilly was in front of him, blocking Tibbett's view.

But Tibbett noticed. "What do you think you are doing? I warned you about that. Back away!"

"Sure," Fargo said, and moved as if he were going to. Instead, he whirled and threw himself onto the bed, tucking into a roll and grabbing his gun belt. The Walker Colt thundered tremendously loud in the confines of the shack and the slug meant for him *thwack*ed into the quilt. Then Fargo was over the other side and palming his revolver as he dropped. Cocking it, he went to shoot, but as quick as he had been, he had not been quick enough.

Tibbett was holding his six-shooter to Tilly's head.

5

First it was a jealous prospector; now it was a drunk one. Fargo had put up with all he was going to. He held his Colt in the air so Tibbett could see it, and said, "Don't shoot her!"

"Then get up from behind there."

Fargo unfurled slowly. He stared hard at Tilly and motioned slightly with his head in the hope she would guess what he was about to do, but she did not seem to notice.

"Set your six-shooter down on the bed," Tibbett directed. "Use two fingers and hold it by the barrel."

Fargo slid his hand along the Colt to do as he had been instructed. "Someone is bound to have heard that shot. People will come to see if she is all right."

Tibbett glanced toward the door. Sure enough, shouts had broken out. He swore, then said, "If anyone knocks, tell them you were cleaning your gun and it went off." As he spoke he wagged the Walker Colt, the muzzle still pointing at Tilly's head.

"What if they insist on talking to Tilly?"

"You damn well better talk them out of it," Tibbett said, swaying anew. "I am not letting go of her and have you jump me. I am too smart for that."

"They might think I shot her," Fargo stalled. "They might not listen to me."

"Damn it, just do as I say!" Tibbett snarled, and for emphasis he jabbed the Walker at him.

It was the moment Fargo had been waiting for. With

a deft flip, he caught his Colt by the grips. He didn't aim. He didn't need to. The target was only a few paces away and as big as a pumpkin.

The lead caught Tibbett in the forehead, angled up through his cranium, and blew out the top of his head in a spectacular spray of gore, hair, bone and blood. He blinked once. Then his legs buckled and he oozed to the floor even as fluid oozed from the bullet hole.

Tilly let out a stifled sob of gratitude and came rushing into Fargo's arms. "Thank you, thank you, thank you!" she gushed. "I thought he was going to kill us."

Fargo savored the warmth and feel of her shapely body. He wanted to explore her contours but boots pounded in the street and a heavy fist pounded on the door.

"Miss Jones? Are you all right? This is Baxter. We heard a shot from your place."

Tilly pried loose and admitted several men. More were outside. She explained and requested that the body be taken away.

Wary glances were thrown at Fargo but no one quizzed him. They accepted the shooting as a fitting fate for anyone who dared threaten a woman. Females were scarce over much of the frontier, especially in hostile territory. Most men treated them with special respect, and woe to the one who didn't.

"We will plant him for you, Miss Jones," Baxter volunteered. He wore a suit and bowler and had a big belly.

Another man had gone through the deceased's pocket. "These are yours if you want them," he said, holding up several dollars. "It is all he had."

Tilly shook her head. "Thank you, but I couldn't take it. I would not feel right." She clasped her arms to her bosom. "Why don't you use it to buy drinks for everyone?"

"You are an angel, Miss Jones," Baxter said.

"Not with my tarnished halo and clipped wings," Tilly replied. "But it is kind of you to say so."

They carried the body out.

Tilly shut and bolted the door, then leaned against it and smiled ruefully at Fargo. "There is nothing like a shooting to spoil the mood. I need to clean up the mess."

"It didn't spoil mine," Fargo said. "And the bed is just fine."

"You are male. The only thing that can spoil a man's mood is to have his redwood chopped off."

Fargo laughed. She had a point.

"Give me a few minutes." Tilly went to the cupboard and took down two glasses and a half-empty whiskey bottle. "Care for a drink?"

"There are two things I never pass up," Fargo bantered. "A pretty filly in a dress and anything in a bottle."

Now it was Tilly who laughed. "This has been some night, hasn't it? You have a knack for attracting people out to kill you."

Her remark gave Fargo pause. It did seem as if every time he turned around someone was out to put holes in his hide. But where there was no law, lawlessness flourished. Shootings and knifings were commonplace. Many towns endured nightly orgies of liquor and violence. Outlaws and badmen of every stripe were as thick as fleas on an old hound.

"Here you go."

Fargo downed his glass at a gulp and enjoyed the warmth that spread down his throat to his belly. "Nice."

"I don't buy cheap whiskey."

"It is not the whiskey I was talking about." Fargo admired the sheen of the lamp light on Tilly's hair, admired, too, the twin mounds that thrust against her dress like ripe melons. The swish of her dress against her legs hinted at velvety delights waiting to be discovered. A lump of raw hunger formed in his throat.

"Are you still fixing to leave tomorrow?" Tilly asked.

"At first light," Fargo said. Out of habit he was nearly always up at the crack of dawn.

"That early?" Tilly sounded disappointed. "Oh, well.

I have to be at the saloon early anyway. A bunch of freight wagons are due in, and those freighters love to drink."

Her mention made Fargo think of Cranmeyer. "Ever hear of the Frazier sisters?"

"Who hasn't? Those girls are the talk of the territory. Mule skinners, like their pa was. Where you find one, you find the other two. They do as they please, when they please, and they don't care who approves."

"You sound as if you admire them."

"You bet your britches I do," Tilly confirmed with a bob of her chin. "What woman wouldn't? They get away with things most of us can only dream of doing." She recited a litany. "They dress like men. They swear like men. They do a man's job better than most men can do it. Above all, they never take guff off of anyone, male or female."

Fargo set his glass on the table. "I like my women to look like women." Placing his hands on her hips, he pulled her to him and kissed her full on the mouth. She melted against him, her fingers plying the hair at the nape of his neck. His skin prickled and he stirred below the belt.

"Lord, what you do to me," Tilly said huskily when the kiss ended. "You have had considerable practice, I suspect."

"A little," Fargo conceded. "But so have you."

"I am the first to admit I like men," Tilly said. "But where a man can be fond of women and nothing much is made of it, when a woman is fond of men she gets a reputation, and the only two places she can find work are a saloon and a sporting house."

"Enough chat," Fargo said, and pulled her close. Their second kiss lasted longer, and when they parted, she was breathing heavily and he had a growing bulge.

Sweeping her into his arms, Fargo carried her to the bed. She grinned as he laid her down on her back.

"Goodness gracious, you work fast."

Fargo went to slide his legs onto the bed and she poked him in the ribs.

"What do you think you are doing? I will thank you to take off your spurs. I already have one hole in my quilt thanks to that idiot Tibbett. I can do without having it torn to shreds."

Fargo couldn't blame her. Quilts took a long time to make. Sitting back up, he removed his right spur and then his left and dropped them to the floor. He also tugged his boots off. Ordinarily he wouldn't bother but they were caked with dirt and except for the bullet holes her bed was immaculate. "Happy now?"

"Very," Tilly said playfully.

Cupping her chin, Fargo fused his mouth to hers. He rekindled his hunger by roving his hands over every square inch of her he could reach. From her shoulders to her knees, he explored her voluptuous womanliness. She responded with rising ardor. Her fingers kneaded his broad shoulders and then roamed across his chest to his flat stomach.

"You have a nice body."

"Not as nice as yours," Fargo said, and nipped another comment in the bud with yet another kiss.

The minutes fluttered by on wings of carnal delight. They probed, caressed, licked and nibbled. Bit by bit her clothes came undone.

Questing fingers roved up under Fargo's buckskin shirt. She plied his skin as if it were clay, and when she came to his waist, she loosened his belt and resumed plying down under. Fargo nearly gasped when she cupped him. The feel of her hand on his pole was almost enough to cause him to explode.

Enrapt in the release of their passion, they drifted on tides of velveteen arousal. Eventually Tilly was as bare as the day she came into the world, and it was not long before Fargo had shed everything but his bandanna. Their lips were everywhere, retracing the explorations of their hands.

Fargo sucked on a hard nipple and Tilly dug her nails so deep into his back, she drew drops of blood. He smacked her bottom and she squirmed and cooed. She cooed so loud and squirmed with such vigor that he smacked her fanny several more times.

"Oh! Oh! I like that!"

Fargo liked how she rimmed his ear with the tip of her tongue and then lightly nipped at his lobe. When she ground against him, he returned the favor. They were hip to hip, chest to breast.

On his knees between her legs, Fargo rubbed his member across her nether lips and elicited a squeal of anticipation. He did not keep her waiting. Inch by inch he fed his iron sword into her satiny moist scabbard. Her ankles locked behind his back and she clamped hold of his arms.

Their eyes met.

"Do me, handsome. Do me good."

Fargo obliged. He rammed and she cried out and each stroke lifted them another rung on the ladder of mutual release. She spurted first, and hers triggered his. The room dissolved around them and there was only the pure, potent pleasure that Fargo could never get enough of.

Still later, the shack was quiet save for Tilly's deep breathing. Fargo tried to join her in slumber but his mind was racing from the events of the evening. He got up and dressed and strapped on his Colt. He figured to write a note but he could not find anything to write with.

Fargo quietly let himself out. The saloon was still open. With a little luck he might find a poker game going, and he could sit in. He crossed the street and was almost to the overhang when a pair of shadows detached themselves from the darkness and barred his way.

"Mr. Fargo! We meet again."

"Hell," Fargo said.

Timothy P. Cranmeyer had a smile worthy of a patent medicine salesman. "We keep running into each other. Some would say that is an omen."

"Or it could be that Hot Springs is no bigger than a gob of spit and a man can't turn around without bumping into someone he doesn't want to bump into." Fargo went to go by but Krupp barred his way. "I am not in the mood. Move or I will move you."

"Now, now," Cranmeyer said. "Hear me out, if you don't mind."

"I already have. Twice. And I will be damned if I will listen a third time." Fargo shouldered past but a hand on his arm stopped him.

"If Mr. Cranmeyer wants you to hear him out, then that is what you will do," Krupp said.

"The wrong night," Fargo told him.

"Eh?"

"You picked the wrong night and the wrong man," Fargo said. "I have been imposed on as much as I am going to be." He did not wait for a response. He hauled off and slugged Krupp flush on the jaw.

The mass of muscle tottered, steadied himself and grinned.

"Not bad."

"I hate this place," Fargo said. Ever since he rode in it had been one thing after another.

"You will hate it more before I am through," Krupp promised, and swung.

Fargo saw the punch coming and threw up an arm to block it. He succeeded, but the blow was so powerful it rocked him onto his boot heels. Raising both fists, he was about to retaliate when Timothy P. Cranmeyer did what he did best—he butted in.

"Hold on, Mr. Krupp! I did not give my consent for you to brawl like a common ruffian."

"Let him," Fargo said. It would serve them right for not leaving him be.

"No, no, no," Cranmeyer said. "I need both of you in good shape for when we reach the mountains."

Fargo was tempted to hit him, too, for the hell of it.

"Mark my words," Cranmeyer said smugly. "I have done some asking around. I know about you. I know what you like more than anything. Tomorrow you will change your mind and agree to join my freight train."

"It must be contagious," Fargo said.

"What?" Cranmeyer asked, puzzled.

"The stupidity." Fargo had had all he could take. He marched into the saloon, determined to drink himself into a stupor. It would help pass the time, if nothing else. Come sunrise, he would be on his way, and if he ever set eyes on Hot Springs again, it would be too soon.

"You will see I am right!" Cranmeyer called from the doorway.

The only thing Fargo wanted to see was a bottle. Nothing, absolutely nothing, could induce him to join a freight train heading up into the stronghold of one of the fiercest tribes on the continent.

Little did he know.

6

The herd of buffalo was endless. The great shaggy brutes came thundering out of the haze and caught Fargo unawares. He lay on the ground, helpless, as their heavy hooves drummed on his skull, over and over and over, an endless pounding that grew to thunder as he struggled to sit up before their flailing hooves crushed him to bits.

Fargo opened his eyes to the harsh glare of the sun and realized it was a dream. He sat up, trying to remember where he was, and the pounding proved to be all too real. His head was spiked by throbbing pain. Squinting, he gazed about him and discovered he was in bed. Specifically, in Tilly's bed, only she wasn't there. He struggled to recall how he wound up back at her place but for the life of him, and the damnable pounding and pain, he couldn't.

Then Fargo saw the empty whiskey bottles on the floor. One was halfway to the bed, the other was next to it. He seemed to vaguely recollect wanting to drink himself into a stupor, and succeeding.

The sunlight streaming in through the window told him he had done something he rarely did; he had slept past sunrise. He shifted to swing his legs over the side and found that he was fully dressed save for his hat, boots and spurs. The former was on the table; the latter were on the floor at the foot of the bed. Tilly's doing, he reckoned, to spare her quilt.

Fargo's mouth was desert dry, and his throat felt as if it was crammed with clinging wool. He coughed but it did no good. He needed something wet to wash the wool down. His teeth clenched against the drumming in his skull. He eased up out of bed and moved toward the cupboard.

Just then the door opened and in bounced Tilly Jones in a green dress with a matching green ribbon in her hair. "Well, look who is up!" she cheerfully exclaimed. "I was beginning to think you would sleep the day away."

Wishing she wouldn't talk so loud, Fargo wet his lips and croaked, "What time is it?"

"It is pushing noon."

Fargo groaned.

"You sure were comical when you showed up about three in the morning," she related. "You were so booze blind, I had to help you into bed and take off your boots."

Fargo nudged the nearest empty bottle with a toe. "Usually two of these is not enough."

"The bartender says you had at least three. He is impressed. He has never seen anyone drink that much and still stay conscious." Tilly cocked her head, studying him. "Why did you do it, anyhow? I thought you wanted to ride out early."

"I did," Fargo said thickly. He had been mad, and fed up, but that was no excuse. It had been plain stupid, and he would kick himself if he had his boots on.

Tilly moved to the stove. "I made coffee before I left. I will heat it for you." She hummed as she worked, saying, "You missed all the excitement. The freight train pulled in a couple of hours ago. Everyone turned out to see them. Ten wagons, loaded with goods for Silver Lode. A fortune's worth, if Tim Cranmeyer can get them up there safely."

"If?" Fargo repeated. He made it to the counter and leaned on it. The number of buffalo dwindled but only for a few seconds.

"The Mimbres Apaches do not like whites traipsing through their mountains," Tilly said, stooping to kindle the embers. "They have attacked nearly every freight train. It is why most freighters won't risk it."

Pressing his hands to his temples, Fargo asked, "What makes Cranmeyer so brave?"

"He needs the money, or so gossip has it. He operates out of Las Cruces. Another man, Jefferson Grind, runs a freighting outfit out of Albuquerque. For some time now there has been bad blood between them. I hear Grind is trying to drive Cranmeyer out of business."

Fargo wondered why Cranmeyer had not mentioned any of that to him. "You're saying this Grind might try to stop Cranmeyer's wagons from reaching Silver Lode?"

"That is what everyone expects, yes," Tilly said, giving the coffeepot a good shake. "Silver Lode needs those provisions. They are willing to pay five times what the goods are worth. And from what I hear, if Cranmeyer doesn't get his wagons there, it could break him."

At last Fargo understood why the man had been so determined to hire him. "What else do you know about Cranmeyer?"

Tilly shrugged. "Not a whole lot. He has a wife and kids tucked away somewhere. Tends to keep to himself. The times he has passed through Hot Springs, he has never once visited the saloon. Word has it he is a teetotaler, if you can believe it."

Fargo opened the cupboard and took down her whiskey bottle. She still had some left, thank God.

"What are you doing? The coffee won't take long to warm."

"To wash down the wool," Fargo said, and chugged. He allowed himself three swallows, then reluctantly set the bottle down and smacked his lips. "Damn, that hits the spot."

"I never took you for a drunk."

"I'm not," Fargo said. He could count the number of times he had drunk himself under the table on two hands and have fingers left over. "But this place was getting to me."

"What you need is to visit the hot springs," Tilly suggested. "Half an hour in that water and you will feel like a new man."

That was not a bad notion, and Fargo said so.

"I go once a week. It clears out the sinuses and makes you feel tingly all over."

Just what Fargo needed—to feel tingly. "I will mosey on over after I have some of your coffee." The buffalo had thinned but a few lingerers were giving his head a hammering.

"I need to get back to the saloon," Tilly said. "It is chock-full of freighters. Two to a wagon, and then there are the outriders."

"Why two?" Fargo inquired. Normally, there was the driver, and that was it.

"Cranmeyer has a rifleman on every wagon. He is not taking any chances if he can help it."

Fargo tallied it up: ten drivers, all undoubtedly armed, ten guards, plus the outriders she mentioned. "He has a small army."

"It might not be enough," Tilly said. "Some of those Mimbres war parties can number a hundred or more."

"Sometimes," Fargo acknowledged. But as a general rule, Apaches prowled in smaller bands, gathering in large numbers on special occasions, as when the prize was worth the extra warriors. And ten wagons laden with goods was quite a prize.

"I hear that Cranmeyer is paying his drivers and guards extra, but I would not go up into those mountains for any amount of money," Tilly remarked. "I am too fond of breathing."

So was Fargo. He stood by his decision to refuse Cranmeyer's offer. The man had plenty of hired protectors. One more would not make that much of a difference.

Tilly came over and draped her hands over his shoulders. "How are you feeling? You look a mite peaked."

"I am fit as a fiddle," Fargo lied.

"I must say, I was surprised when you banged on my door and woke me up. I barely got you to bed. You couldn't hardly stand without my help."

"I am obliged."

"Oh, pshaw. It is not as if we were strangers." Tilly

winked and turned to the stove. "The coffee will be ready in a bit."

Fargo would rather have more whiskey but he humored her. Besides, the coffee would clear his head for the long ride he had ahead.

"Want some eggs and bacon, too?"

The mere thought of food made Fargo's stomach try to crawl up his throat. Shaking his head, he moved to the window. Freight wagons lined the street from end to end. The teams were mules, not oxen, which made sense given that although oxen were stronger and hardier, mules were faster, and in Apache country speed counted far more than strength. The quicker Cranmeyer reached Silver Lode, the less time he and his wagons spent on the trail, and the higher the likelihood he would get there alive.

Just then Fargo spied Cranmeyer and Krupp over by one of the wagons. He remembered Cranmeyer saying how he would change his mind about accompanying the freight train, and chuckled.

"What do you see?" Tilly inquired.

"A gent who is a flop at predicting the future." Fargo gazed at the enclosure over the hot springs. After his coffee he would mosey on over and sweat the liquor out of his system.

"Any sign of the triplets?"

"The who?" Fargo responded.

"The Frazier girls. The mule skinners. They are as alike as three peas in a pod. Wherever they go, they are an attraction. Men drool and the womenfolk are jealous."

"Does that include you?" Fargo teased.

"I admit I feel a pang of green," Tilly revealed. "God saw fit to grace them with uncommon beauty."

"You are an eyeful yourself."

"Why, thank you, kind sir," Tilly said with self-deprecating humor. "But I know my limitations. And I am telling you those three are as perfect as the female form can be."

"I will believe it when I see one," Fargo said offhandedly.

"Most likely you will find them over at the saloon. That is where they usually deport themselves."

"You don't say," Fargo said. Except for doves like Tilly, most females avoided saloons as if afraid to step through the batwings for fear of coming down with a case of bad morals.

"I know you do not believe me but you will when you see them. They are an eyeful and then some."

"I have met a lot of eyefuls," Fargo told her.

Tilly looked up from the stove. "Not like those three. All that beauty, yet they hold their own with men."

"There you go again."

"For better or worse, this is pretty much a man's world. I mean, men control things, don't they? More than they should, if you ask me. But be that as it may, the Frazier girls have done what most women only dream of doing. They are equal to men in every respect."

The feeling in her voice surprised him.

"I would love to be as they are but I lack the gumption. I am content doing what I do."

Fargo walked over and kissed her on the cheek. "You won't hear me complain."

Grinning, Tilly returned the favor. "I don't expect you to understand. You are a man. You have never been treated as women are treated. We are second-rate citizens. Hell, we don't even have the right to vote."

"I could really use that coffee," Fargo said.

Tilly laughed. "See? You are a typical male. You don't even want to hear what I have to say."

"I am a male with an avalanche between my ears," Fargo set her straight, "and I want it to stop."

"Serves you right," Tilly teased, and then stiffened when loud knocking shook the front door.

"Expecting company?" Fargo asked.

Shaking her head, Tilly went over but she did not open it. "Who's there?" she nervously demanded.

"The name is Krupp, Miss Jones. I work for Tim Cranmeyer."

"What do you want?"

"Mr. Cranmeyer sent me to talk to your guest. I cannot go until I have, so please, make this easy and have him come to the door. I promise that I mean him no harm."

"My guest?" Tilly said.

"We know Fargo spent the night with you but that is neither here nor there. What you do is your own affair. All Mr. Cranmeyer wants is a few words with him."

Fargo saw no sense in pretending not to be there. "Go pester someone else. I told your boss before and I am telling you now that I am not interested."

"He says it is important."

"Not to me," Fargo said.

"I will wait out here until you show yourself and then I will take you to him," Krupp informed him.

Fargo did not like the sound of that. Striding to the door, he yanked it open. "You are welcome to try," he said.

"I have no interest in fighting you," Krupp assured him. "I am only doing what I was told."

"Keep on doing it," Fargo said. "Let your boss know that if he bothers me one more time, there will be hell to pay."

"You can let him know yourself," Krupp said, and motioned. "After you, if you don't mind."

"I do," Fargo said. He was fast losing his patience. "Now scat, you big lump."

Krupp let out a sigh. "Mr. Cranmeyer said you would say that. He also said you would take special convincing." Raising his arm, he snapped his fingers. "I envy you."

"What the hell are you babbling—" Fargo began, and caught himself as astonishment flooded through him. He looked, and blinked, and said the first thing that popped into his head. "I'll be damned."

7

Fargo had known a lot of women in his time. A *lot* of women. In the biblical sense, as he had gotten to know Tilly Jones. Of the top three things he enjoyed most in life, women were one, two and three. He liked the feel of them, the smell of them, the sound of them. He liked to join his body to theirs and pound them until they gushed.

Fate had favored him in that women found him attractive. When he looked in the mirror he saw an ordinary man with ordinary features, but women had told him he was handsome so many times, he had lost count. He never regarded himself as special but the ladies sure did.

Short women, tall women, slender women, women who were pleasantly full-bodied. Redheads, brunettes, raven-haired lovelies, sandy-headed vixens and women with every color in between. White women, Indian maidens, Oriental gals, females of every hue there was.

He had been with them all.

Their looks never mattered all that much. If a woman's nose was too big or she had no chin to speak of, or whether her legs were long and willowy or short and thin, or even if her mounds were huge or small, was of no consequence.

Most were pretty in one way or another. Some were lovely. A few were downright beautiful. Perhaps half a dozen had been exquisite.

But Fargo had never, ever, set his eyes on a vision of absolute perfection—until now.

The three women who came strolling toward him wore the coarse clothes typical of those in their line of work. Their shirts were homespun, their pants and belts commonplace, their boots scuffed. But there was nothing coarse or common or scuffed about *them*. Despite their clothes, they were as beautiful as women could be, or ever hope to be.

Even more remarkably, they were identical in every respect. Not a shade of difference existed between them, except that one wore a brown shirt, one wore black and the third's shirt was striped.

Their hair was a unique mix of red and copper and shimmered like burnished metal. Their eyebrows were arched, their noses were finely aquiline, their lips red and full, but not too full. Their eyes were a piercing green that seemed to dance with inner flames.

When they moved, they were grace in motion, smooth and fluid, yet unassuming.

In short, the triplets were superb in every facet, human diamonds without flaw.

"I would like you to meet the Frazier sisters," Krupp said, and grinned.

The trio was remarkable in another respect. Most women went around unarmed. But not the Fraziers. Each wore a revolver and a belt knife and held a coiled bullwhip. Something about the way they held those whips suggested they were extremely adept at wielding them.

All three grinned, showing teeth as dazzling white as polished pearls.

Then the vision in the brown shirt said, "What do we have here, sisters?"

"I do declare," said the one in black. "We have struck the mother lode."

The one in the striped shirt looked Fargo up and down. "We will have to draw lots."

All Fargo could do was stare. Their voices were as perfect as the rest of them, almost musical in pitch and tone, yet convening a sensual quality that set a man's spine to tingling.

"It looks as if the cat has his tongue," joked Brown Shirt.

"Lucky cat," said Black Shirt.

Striped Shirt laughed. "You would think he had been kicked in the head by a mule."

Fargo, for one of the few times in his life, was still speechless with wonderment.

Krupp was taking delight in the situation. "You must forgive him, ladies. From what I hear, it is the first time he has ever set eyes on you."

"We do tend to have an effect, don't we?" bantered Brown Shirt.

"It is not our fault," said the black-shirted triplet. "We were born this way."

Striped Shirt nodded. "Life is like cards. We are dealt what we are dealt and must make the best of it."

With a toss of his head, Fargo broke their spell. "So you are the Fraziers. I can see why everyone makes such a fuss." He looked at Krupp. "But it doesn't change a thing. Tell your boss it didn't work."

Krupp acted as if he had not heard. "Let me introduce them." He pointed at the triplet in brown. "This is Myrtle." At the triplet in black. "This is Mavis." At the triplet in the striped shirt. "And this is Cleopatra."

Fargo could not help himself. He snorted in amusement. "Cleopatra?"

The third sister flashed those white teeth of hers. "Our ma was partial to the name. She heard about a queen somewhere who had it once."

"Egypt," Myrtle said. "The country was Egypt. How many times must I remind you?"

"Don't start," Cleopatra said. "I don't care where it was. I have never liked the name and never will. Ma made me a laughingstock. I would rather have a name that begins with an M, like you and Mavis, and Ma herself."

"You have it backward," Mavis said. "Our family has been giving girls names with an M for as long as I can remember. Myrtle. Me. Ma was Margaret. Her sister was

Mary. Her sister's girls were Milly and May. Our cousins were Marjorie, Marigold, Matty and Minny. It is stupid. I would give anything to have a name like yours. A name that does not begin with an M."

Krupp gestured. "Enough. We are not here to talk about names. I have heard this bickering before and I am tired of it."

As one, the three sisters stared at him. As one, each held her bullwhip in front of her at waist height.

"I don't know as I like your tone," Myrtle said.

"Me either," Mavis echoed.

Cleopatra gave her bullwhip a sharp shake. "No one tells us what to do. Ever. Do you need a reminder?"

Fargo was puzzled to see Krupp take a step back and hold up both hands, palms out. The man had stood up to him—yet he was wary of tangling with the triplets.

"Now you just hold on, Cleo. I have always respected you gals and you know it."

Cleopatra frowned but lowered her whip. "Yes, Captain, you have. But I still did not like your tone. My sisters and me have had to scrabble hard to make it in this world, and we will not be slighted on account of our being women."

"When have I ever?" Krupp countered. "I made the three of you my lieutenants, didn't I?"

Fargo was familiar with how freighters were organized. Each train had a captain and usually a couple of lieutenants who passed on his orders and helped ensure things went as they should. The drivers took turns watching over the animals at night, although on some trains, a man was chosen as night wrangler and had the job for the duration.

"I would never treat you any different than I do the men," Krupp was assuring the sisters. "Now please. You were sent over here for a purpose, remember?"

All three switched those dazzling green eyes of theirs from the captain to Fargo.

"We hear that Mr. Cranmeyer wants you to join our train," Cleopatra said softly, coming closer.

"But for some reason you told him no," Myrtle huskily mentioned, doing the same.

"What can we do to get you to say yes?" Mavis asked, and hefted her bullwhip.

Fargo smothered a laugh. He could not decide if they were threatening him or appealing to the part of a man that needed no convincing where women were concerned.

"You don't say a lot," Cleopatra said.

Fargo disagreed. "I do when I have something to say. I told Cranmeyer, I told Krupp, and now I am telling you. I am not going with you."

"What if we make it worth your while?" From Myrtle.

"How?"

Myrtle touched her coiled whip to his hip and slowly ran it down to his knee. "Can't you guess?"

Fargo's confusion climbed. One minute they were going on about how they were struggling for respect in a man's world; the next they were practically throwing themselves at him. It made no sense. "If that is all, ladies," he said, and started to back through the doorway.

"Hold on," Mavis said, clutching his hand. "We are not accustomed to a man saying no."

"Hell, I don't even know what I said no to," Fargo said, twisting loose.

"Why won't you lend Mr. Cranmeyer a hand?" Myrtle asked. "He says that he is willing to pay you extra. More, in fact, than he is paying anyone else."

"Why is that?" Cleopatra wanted to know.

"What makes you so special?" Mavis chimed in.

Krupp cleared his throat. "I can answer that one, ladies. Fargo, here, has done a lot of scouting for the army. He has fought redskins more times than all our drivers and guards put together and lived to tell the tale."

"You don't say," Myrtle said, impressed.

"Not only that," Krupp continued, "but he has fought *Apaches*. Even better, he has been in the Mimbres Mountains a few times. He knows the trails, the water holes."

Fargo's brow knit in perplexity. "And how is it you know all that?"

"I wasn't always a freight captain," Krupp said.

Mavis touched her whip to Fargo's chest. "It sounds to me like you are just the gent we need."

"Mr. Cranmeyer thinks so," Krupp told her. "He told me that whether we make it or not could depend on having Fargo along."

"One more gun won't make much of a difference," Fargo said.

"It is not your gun; it is *you*," Krupp responded. "Or are you going to stand there and deny you have met Cuchillo Negro?"

All three sisters betrayed their surprise.

While not as influential among his people as the likes of Mangus Colorado or Ponce, Cuchillo Negro led a band of some thirty to forty warriors who routinely conducted raids both north and south of the border. It was true Fargo had run into him before—but it was not common knowledge.

"That devil has been acting up of late," Cleopatra said. "If you know him, you owe it to us to talk him into leaving our train alone."

"The last time I saw Cuchillo Negro, he was trying to kill me." Fargo had been lucky to escape intact.

"It can't hurt to have you along," Krupp insisted. "We leave in a couple of hours. You have until then to decide."

Fargo wheeled and nearly collided with Tilly, who was gawking at the triplets. She moved out of his way and he went over to the stove. The coffee was hot. He filled a cup to the brim with the steaming black cure for his hammering head and took several loud sips, then turned, expecting to find Tilly had closed the door. But she was gone and the door was still open and the Frazier sisters were filing in. "Where did Tilly get to?"

"She said she had to get back to work," Myrtle replied.

"Did she invite you in?"

"We are not done persuading you," Mavis said.

"Yes, you are." Fargo had his limits and this had gone on long enough. So what if they were the finest females he'd ever come across? They were not enough to induce him to give in. "I have had my say and it is final."

Cleopatra came up and lightly touched a fingertip to his chin. "Women always have the last word, not men."

"I wish you were men," Fargo said. So he could chuck them out in the street.

"Now, now," Myrtle said, placing a warm hand on his arm. "What can it hurt to hear our special proposition?"

Fargo swallowed more coffee. "What makes it so special?"

Mavis tittered and her sisters followed suit. "Because the only one we are making it to is you." She and her siblings glanced at one another and grinned and nodded. "I think you will like it. I think you will like it so much that you will change your mind and agree to help guard our freight train."

"Don't any of you listen?" Fargo growled in exasperation. "There is nothing you can do or say that will change my mind."

"Oh, really?" Mavis said. And just like that, she raised his hand to her bosom and placed it on her right breast.

A lump formed in Fargo's throat. She had nothing on under the black shirt. He could feel the fullness of her mound, feel her nipple against his palm. He quickly gulped more coffee. "What the hell are you playing at?"

Grinning mischievously, Mavis removed his hand from her breast but did not let go of his fingers. "If you knew us well enough, you would know we never play when it comes to this."

"To what?"

It was Myrtle who answered. "To bedding men. We are particular about who we share our bodies with. We do not jump in the hay with just anyone. We have what you might call standards."

"All three of us have to like him," Cleopatra elaborated when her sister stopped. "Sometimes only one of us will like him. Sometimes two of us will think he is gorgeous but the third one can't be bothered. Then there are men who excite all three of us. Men who excite us terribly."

"Which brings us to you," Mavis said.

Ever since Fargo rode into Hot Springs, it had been one thing after another. The stupid prospector. The drunk prospector. Cranmeyer refusing to take no for an answer. Now this. "I excite you?"

"I could eat you alive," Mavis said.

"We are going to make you an offer no man in his right mind would refuse," Myrtle declared.

Cleopatra made it plain. "Join up with our freight train you can have your way with all three of us."

"Oh, hell," Skye Fargo said.

8

The ten wagons creaked and clattered and rattled, spewing a thick cloud of dust into the hot summer sky.

Fargo twisted in the saddle, and frowned. That dust could be seen for miles. But he was not overly concerned. They were only one day out of Hot Springs. It would be a few more days yet before they reached the Mimbres Mountains. *That* was when he could really start to worry.

Then again, Fargo reflected as he gigged the Ovaro, Apaches were notoriously unpredictable. They could strike anywhere. Attacks this close to a settlement were rare but Fargo had learned the hard way never to take anything for granted. Especially when dealing with Apaches.

Unlike most whites, who hated Indians in general and Apaches most of all, Fargo had a genuine respect for their hardy natures and warrior way of life. They were fierce and free and determined to stay that way.

Lords and masters over a vast area that included some of the harshest terrain on the planet, for centuries the Apaches had raided and plundered at will. Other tribes lived in constant fear of them. Mexican authorities were offering bounties for their scalps in an effort to exterminate them. Not all that long ago, Spain tried to claim Apache territory for its own and failed spectacularly.

Now the white man was trying to do what the other tribes and the Spaniards and the Mexicans could not. The whites were out to defeat a people who would not bend their knee to anyone, ensuring there would be bloodshed, and a lot of it.

The thud of the Ovaro's hooves intruded on Fargo's reverie. He slowed as he came up alongside the first wagon and glanced at Timothy P. Cranmeyer. Cranmeyer was handling the team himself, and handling it well. Krupp sat beside him, a rifle across his lap. "We are making good time."

Cranmeyer smirked. That smirk had been a fixture ever since Fargo walked up to him in the saloon and said that he was willing to help get the train to Silver Lode. "You rode up to tell me something I already know?"

"Tilly Jones told me that you have been squabbling with a gent by the name of Grind," Fargo mentioned.

The smirk vanished. "It is far more than squabbling. It is open war. Jefferson Grind is intent on driving me out of business."

"How about you?"

"I am not sure I understand," Cranmeyer said, and coughed as dust speckled his face.

"Is it one-sided?"

"I was in business first, Mr. Fargo. I started my freight company two and a half years ago and was doing quite well until Jefferson Grind came along and set up his own firm."

"You didn't answer my question."

Cranmeyer shifted on the seat. "As God is my witness, I did not start this. Grind did. Some of my wagons were set on fire in the middle of the night. I went to talk to him and asked if he had a hand in it, and he denied he was to blame. But he was lying."

"How do you know?"

"I could tell just by looking at him. That, and rumors my men picked up here and there. Grind's drivers were boasting that Grind intended to drive me under. That sort of thing."

As if having the Apaches to deal with was not enough, Fargo had put himself smack in the middle of a bitter business feud. "How far is Grind willing to go? Has anyone died in this little war of yours?"

"Not yet. So far he has been content with destroying my assets and sabotaging my runs, but I would not put anything past him."

Fargo remembered Tilly saying something about Cranmeyer needing money to stay afloat. "And if this train doesn't get through?"

"I will be in dire straits," Cranmeyer admitted. "The war with Grind has drained my resources. Unless I have an infusion of cash I might go under."

"Is that why you are handling this wagon yourself?" Fargo asked. Normally, freight company presidents left the driving to the mule skinners or bullwhackers.

"You are most perceptive, Mr. Fargo," Cranmeyer complimented him. "Yes, that is exactly why. I desperately need the money Silver Lode is willing to pay for these provisions. I cannot sit idly by while my livelihood hangs in the balance."

Krupp chose that moment to straighten and say, "Don't you worry, Mr. Cranmeyer. We will get these wagons through no matter what. I stake my life on it."

"Let us hope, my dear Krupp, that so severe a sacrifice is not called for," Cranmeyer said.

Fargo used his spurs and trotted a hundred yards to where a pair of heavily armed outriders was on point. The taller of the two, who had been introduced to him as Ezekiel Stack, favored a broad-brimmed hat and a pearl-handled Remington. Stack gave a curt nod.

"Do you want something?"

Fargo did not know what to make of him. Cranmeyer had hired the man only recently, paying top dollar, because Stack was supposed to be uncommonly good with that fancy Remington. But Stack was as friendly as a rattler and stayed aloof from everyone. "Keep your eyes peeled. The Apaches are not the only ones who might try to stop us."

"I know about Grind," Stack said. "I will not lose any sleep over him."

"You don't care because these aren't your wagons—is that it?" Fargo probed.

"I will not lose any sleep because if any of Grind's outfit give us trouble, they will answer to this." Grind patted the Remington.

"You like to squeeze the trigger."

"I could carve more than a few notches if I was vain enough," Stack said. "That is why Cranmeyer hired me. You, too, for that matter. He needs curly wolves like us to get these wagons through."

"Ever done any Indian fighting?"

Stack took off his hat and indicated a four-inch scar high on his brow, almost at the hairline. "See this? Courtesy of a Chiricahua who was out to scalp me. He would have, too, if I hadn't shoved my six-gun between his legs and put two into his groin."

Fargo was impressed. The Chiricahuas were as formidable as the Mimbres. Few whites survived a clash with them. "I am going on ahead. If I am not back in a couple of hours, stop the train and send someone to look for me."

"I will look myself," Stack said. "I am the only one I trust to do things right."

The burning sun, the dry air, lent Fargo the illusion of being in an oven. He loosened his bandanna and resisted an urge to resort to his canteen. Water was scarce and would be more so when they reached the mountains.

Once around a bend he had the country to himself. He liked it that way. He could think without distractions, and he had a lot to ponder. Foremost was his decision to join the train.

Fargo recollected hearing once about a book that had to do with the ancient Greeks, and a city called Troy. A Greek hero who was supposed to be invincible—Achilles—died when an arrow pierced his heel. Ever since, every man's greatest weakness was his Achilles' heel.

His was women.

The Frazier sisters had done it. They brazenly made

him an offer that appealed to his weakness, and God help him, he gave in. He could no more refuse their charms than a drunk could refuse a drink or an opium addict could pass by an opium den.

Fargo was not very pleased with himself.

But the next moment he forgot all about the triplets. Tendrils of dust were rising a half mile away. He watched closely and established that whoever or whatever was raising the dust was on the road, and coming in his direction. Odds were they were white, not red. Indians disdained roads as they did so much of the white world. And, too, the road was the main link between Hot Springs and the high country. Travelers used it daily.

Fargo kept on riding, holding to a walk to spare the Ovaro. He did not think much of it when four riders appeared. They were, as he had guessed they would be, white. They were armed, but so was everyone in that country. Their clothes were the ordinary variety that any rancher or anyone else who spent a lot of time outdoors would wear.

Then Fargo drew closer. He noted their hard, predatory faces, and how they rode with hands close to their revolvers and sat their saddles with slightly tense postures. He drew rein at the edge of the road, leaned on his saddle horn, and nodded in greeting. "How do you do, gents."

The four came to a stop. Neither they nor their mounts were caked with dust, as they would be if they had ridden any distance. In fact, in Fargo's opinion, they could not have been on the road more than an hour.

A short man in the middle scratched his salt-and-pepper stubble and nodded in return. "Howdy, stranger. On your way from Hot Springs, I see."

"Heading for Silver Lode," Fargo said. "And I was wondering if you have heard of any Indian trouble between here and there."

"We did not come down from the mountains," the man said. "But we hear tell that a Mimbres war party has been causing folks misery."

"You don't say," Fargo responded. "Did you come from the north or the south?"

The last man on the other side snapped his head up. "What business is it of yours?"

Venting a sigh, the short man said, "Pay him no mind, mister. He was born with a sour disposition. We are from Albuquerque, bound for Hot Springs."

Fargo idly slid his hands off his saddle horn and lowered them to his sides. His right hand brushed his holster. "A couple of men were killed there last night. Prospectors."

"You don't say," the talkative one replied, and leaned on his own saddle horn. "You didn't happen to see anything of a freight train while you were there, did you? We hear one might be passing through this area, and we need to find it."

"As a matter of fact," Fargo answered, "there is one about a half mile back. If you wait a spell they will be here soon enough." He placed his left hand on his hip and his right hand on his Colt. "Are you hunting up some freight?"

"Not exactly, no," the short man said, and lifted his reins to depart. "I am obliged for the information. Watch out for those Mimbres when you get up in the high country."

"One bridge at a time," Fargo said. "First I have to cross this one."

The man on the other side of the road snorted. "What in hell are you talking about? You won't find a bridge within a hundred miles."

"There are four bridges," Fargo said, and nodded at each of the riders in turn. "That is, if my hunch is right, and the four of you work for an hombre by the name of Jefferson Grind."

The effect was instantaneous. All four of them went rigid, and four hands edged closer to four holsters.

"What is Jefferson Grind to you?" the friendly one asked.

"He is out to ruin a freight company run by Timothy P. Cranmeyer," Fargo said.

"Let me rephrase that, then," the short man said. "What is Cranmeyer to you? And how is it you know about their feud?"

"Cranmeyer told me. He is paying me to see that all his wagons reach Silver Lode."

"Well," the short man said, and glanced at his companions.

"I don't suppose you would be willing to turn around and ride back to Albuquerque?" Fargo asked.

"Not if we want to be paid."

"You would die for a few hundred?" Fargo tried again.

"Five hundred is more than a few."

"For each of you?"

The short man nodded.

Fargo whistled. That made for a total of two thousand dollars. "Jefferson Grind must have money to spare."

"More than you or me will ever see. And we are only four of the fifteen he has hired."

The rider at the other end took exception. "You talk too damn much, Wilson. If this Daniel Boone has hired out to Cranmeyer, why are we sitting here flapping our gums when we should be filling him with lead?"

"I am in no hurry to die," Wilson said.

"Hell, there are four of us and only one of him. I say we turn him into worm food and be done with it."

Wilson looked at him. "In case you have forgotten, Grind put me in charge. None of you are to touch your hardware until I say to. Is that understood, Becker?"

"To hell with that and to hell with you," Becker said, and swooped his hand to his revolver.

So did Fargo. He had his Colt up and out before Becker cleared leather. He fired from the hip, forced to rush his shot before the others went for their hardware. His slug caught Becker high on the forehead and snapped Becker's head back as if it had been kicked by a mule.

Instantly, Fargo swiveled.

The other three were drawing. Wilson almost had his revolver unlimbered. Fargo fired twice into Wilson's chest, shot the third man as his arm was rising, and shot the last leather slapper as the man's six-shooter went off.

The last man missed.

Fargo didn't.

In the sudden silence one of their horses bolted.

Dismounting, Fargo stepped up to Wilson, who was on his back, gulping air like a fish out of water. "It did not have to be this way."

"Yes, it did."

"Another time, another place," Fargo said.

Wilson's mouth quirked upward. "Any chance you can bury me? I don't cotton ending up as buzzard shit."

"The buzzards can eat the others."

"Thank you." Gasping in pain, Wilson convulsed, then sank back, saying, "I want to return the favor. You better watch out. Jefferson Grind has an ace up his sleeve. Something you would never expect."

"I am listening."

Wilson went to speak, and died.

9

Fargo was adding a few last rocks to the pile when the wagons lumbered into view. The other three bodies lay in a row at the side of the road. They could rot there, for all he cared. Removing his hat, he wiped his face and neck with his bandanna, then retired the bandanna and stood next to the Ovaro to await the freight train.

Ezekiel Stack and the rest of the outriders spotted him and came on ahead in a group. Stack stared hard at the dead men, particularly the one called Becker, and said, "Some of Grind's men, I take it?"

It was the logical conclusion. Or was it? Fargo wondered. From the way Stack stared at them, it was almost as if he knew them. Fargo recalled Wilson saying that Jefferson Grind had an ace up his sleeve. Could that ace be someone on Cranmeyer's payroll, but who was secretly working for Grind? And could that someone be Stack?

Presently, the wagons arrived, and everyone gathered to inspect the bodies and hear Fargo's account of the affray. He kept it short and left out the part about the ace up Grind's sleeve.

Cranmeyer stood over the bodies with his hands clasped behind his back and said to Krupp. "See? I told you Mr. Fargo was worth his weight in silver. His reputation is well deserved."

Krupp frowned and said, "These four are just the start. There will be more."

The Frazier sisters were huddled by themselves, whispering. When Fargo glanced at them, all three smiled sweetly and Cleopatra, the brazen hussy, moved her legs suggestively.

Fargo stayed with the wagon train the rest of the day. He constantly roved from point to the rear, keeping an eye out for more of Grind's hired killers. Once an elderly couple in a buckboard came by. Another time it was a patent medicine salesman in a van.

Sunset found them camped a few dozen yards to the north of the road. The freight wagons were in a circle, the mules tethered and under the watchful eye of a nighthawk. Two crackling fires blazed, one on the north side of the circle, the other on the south.

A black man was preparing supper. Apparently he had worked as a cook in a restaurant until Cranmeyer hired him to do the same for the freight firm.

All the precautions that could be taken had been taken.

For the first time since they started out from Hot Springs, Fargo could relax. He sat cross-legged in the shadow of a wagon and nursed a cup of coffee, his Henry beside him.

Boots crunched, and Stack was there. "Anything else you need me to do?" he inquired.

Fargo hoped he was wrong about him. "Not at the moment, no. Except maybe remind the wrangler that if he falls asleep and we lose mules to the Apaches or anyone else, he will be walking on crutches for a while."

Stack smiled. "I will pass it on. But don't worry. Frank is a good man. Cranmeyer only hires men he can trust to get the job done."

"I hope so," Fargo said.

About to go, Stack paused. "There is something I should tell you. I knew one of those men you shot. His name was Becker."

Fargo hid his surprise at the admission. "Knew him how?"

"He has been drifting around the territory for a few

years now, hiring out his pistol. I have been doing the same. We worked together once about six months ago."

"Was he a friend of yours?" Fargo asked.

"An acquaintance, is all, and not one I was fond of," Stack said. "Becker was hard to get along with. He always had a burr up his ass about something or other."

"So you don't hold shooting him against me?"

"You did what you had to. I would have done the same if I was in your boots." Stack touched his hat brim and walked off.

Fargo went back to sipping his coffee but he was not alone for long. Three winsome forms, bullwhips in hand, made him the envy of the camp by coming over to see him.

"That sure was something, what you did today," Myrtle Frazier said.

"Gunning down four at once!" Mavis marveled. "You must be lightning with that six-shooter of yours."

Cleopatra, always the vixen, grinned. "I hope you don't do *everything* fast. Some things deserve to be done slow."

"Have something special in mind?" Fargo asked.

"As if you can't guess," Cleopatra replied, and laughed that husky laugh of hers. Her sisters joined in.

Fargo leaned against the wagon wheel and regarded them with keen interest. "Who is to be first?"

"I beg your pardon?" Mavis replied.

"Don't play innocent," Fargo said. "We have a deal. I joined the freight train, so I get to have all three of you."

Myrtle frowned in disapproval. "You do not need to be crude about it."

"Goodness, no," Mavis said. "Only you do not get to set the time and the place. We do."

"You aren't trying to weasel out on me, are you?"

All three flushed with anger. Cleopatra bent down, crooked a finger, and hooked her fingernail under his chin. "If you weren't so damn good-looking, I would take my whip to you."

"So would I," Myrtle said. "We always keep our word. Ask anyone."

Mavis nodded. "When we say we will do something, we will do it."

"But we are not common tarts," Cleopatra added, lightly sliding her finger along his jaw to his ear. "We do not spread our legs for every male we see. We choose carefully. And when we do share ourselves, we like to do the deed in private."

"Do you have a problem with that?" Mavis demanded.

"Not at all, ladies," Fargo assured them. "I don't care if we do it in a wagon or off in the desert or in a ditch. Just so we do it. And since it will be harder to find time to ourselves once we are in the mountains, now is as good a time as any."

"My, oh, my, aren't you the randy?" Cleopatra teased. "But then, all men are. You can't help yourselves. You are born that way."

"Slaves to your peckers," Myrtle said sagely.

"Not that we are complaining," Mavis threw in. "A man's pecker is a like a nose ring on a bull. All a savvy gal has to do is take hold of it and the man is in her power."

"My pecker is not a nose ring," Fargo enlightened them.

"Oh, please," Cleopatra said. "All men ever think of is one thing. I have never met a man yet who did not have his brains below his belt."

"That is harsh."

"Don't take it personal. Like Mavis just told you, you won't hear us complain. We are fond of peckers, ourselves."

Fargo laughed.

"As for your notion that now is as good a time as any," Cleopatra went on, "give us a minute or two and we will get back to you."

They went out of earshot of him and everyone else, and huddled. From their expressions and how they kept shaking their bullwhips at one another, they appeared to be arguing, and arguing heatedly.

Fargo had no inkling what it was about. Cranmeyer had noticed and did not look happy, probably because a lot of the drivers and guards had noticed, too.

Mavis fished in her pants and produced a coin. She flipped it high into the air and let it land at her feet. All three bent to see which side of the coin was up. Then Myrtle flipped it. Then Cleopatra took her turn.

Smoothing her shirt, Myrtle sashayed back to Fargo. She was grinning from ear to ear.

"Guess what, handsome?"

"You won."

Myrtle nodded enthusiastically. "That is how we decide. We take turns tossing the coin so it is fair."

"What if I want one of the others?" Fargo asked, and chuckled at her crestfallen expression. "I was joshing. The three of you look so much alike, it doesn't matter."

"Ah, but it does," Myrtle disagreed. "Looks are not everything. We might seem to be as alike as like can be, but we are each of us different. Cleo is a wildcat when she is with a man. Mavis hardly ever does more than kiss and fondle until the deed is done."

"And you?"

"Me?" Myrtle said, and showed her pearly teeth. "I like to give as good as I get, if you catch my meaning."

"Prove it," Fargo said.

Myrtle gestured at the campfires and the men. "In private, remember?" She touched his knee with her bullwhip. "Why don't we go for a stroll and I will prove I am as I say I am?"

Fargo drained his tin cup and pushed to his feet. "A stroll happens to be just what I need."

"I'll bet."

Fargo linked arms with her. "I am looking forward to this." He was not exaggerating; he was curious to learn whether the parts of the Frazier sisters he could not see were as gloriously perfect as the parts he could.

"So am I, handsome," Myrtle admitted. "I know it is

not proper for a lady to confess to carnal desires, but I refuse to go through life pretending to be someone I am not."

"I don't blame you." Fargo made small talk while admiring the twin peaks that poked at her shirt.

They had taken only a few steps when someone came up behind them. Timothy P. Cranmeyer was without Krupp for once. His hands were behind his back, as was his habit, and he nervously rocked on his heels. "Pardon me, Mr. Fargo. But might I have a few words with you?"

Fargo glanced at Myrtle, who shrugged to show she had no idea what Cranmeyer wanted. "So long as the words are few."

Cranmeyer smiled and motioned for Fargo to walk beside him.

"This better be important," Fargo grumbled. He had his mind, and body, fixed on one thing, and he did not appreciate the interruption.

"It is," Cranmeyer said. When they were a fair distance from Myrtle and everyone else, he stopped and bowed his head and commenced rocking on his heels again. "This comes hard for me."

"What does?"

"Intruding where I have no right to intrude. But I must do what is best for the good of all."

"You are taking the long way around the stable to get your horse in the stall," Fargo said drily.

"Very well." Cranmeyer coughed and finally met his gaze. "I would take it as a personal favor if you would refrain from indulging your physical urges until we reach Silver Lode."

"I should shoot you," Fargo said.

"Excuse me?"

"You are the one who sicced the Fraziers on me, remember? To convince me to change my mind? Well, they did, and here I am, and here they are, and if they want to go on convincing, by God I will let them."

Cranmeyer glanced at Myrtle, then toward Cleopatra and Mavis. "If only they weren't three of the best mule skinners in the business I would have nothing to do with them."

"That is between them and you."

"True," Cranmeyer said. "But what goes on between them and *you* can cause all sorts of trouble for *me*. Trouble I could do without."

"Spell it out," Fargo said.

"Since you insist." Cranmeyer paused. "I doubt it has escaped your notice that they are three of the loveliest women on God's green earth. They turn heads everywhere they go."

"They turned mine," Fargo said.

"I was hoping they would," Cranmeyer admitted. "But now that they have, it wouldn't do to give the impression they are partial to you over everyone else."

"The hell you say."

"Every man here would love to get his hands on them. I have made it clear the Fraziers are off-limits, and the men have smothered their urges. But they will not keep those urges smothered if they see you carrying on as if you have your own personal harem."

Fargo saw where it was leading, and swore.

"Please. All I ask is that you hold off until we reach Silver Lode. Once we are there you can do as you please."

"You are making a mountain out of a prairie dog mound."

"I have enough problems," Cranmeyer said. "What with the Apaches on the warpath and Jefferson Grind out to get me and creditors camped in front of my house. I do not need for my men to kill one another in fits of jealously."

"Silver Lode?" Fargo said.

"Yes, just until there," Cranmeyer said hopefully. "Do I have your word?"

Fargo stared at Cleopatra and Mavis, then at Myrtle, who was impatiently tapping her foot. Three of the most exquisite females he ever met, each the kind of woman a man remembered for the rest of his born days.

"Well?" Cranmeyer prompted.

"Let me put it this way," Fargo said, and sought to soften the blow by placing his hand on Cranmeyer's shoulder, and smiling. "There isn't a snowball's chance in hell."

"You insist on making love to them?"

"That is a god-awful stupid question."

Cranmeyer was not amused. "Fine. But I must say, I am disappointed. I expected better of you."

"It is your own fault," Fargo said.

"Me? What did I do?"

"You should hire uglier mule skinners."

10

Myrtle was fidgeting when Fargo returned. "What was that all about?" she asked.

Fargo had no reason not to tell her. He did, thinking she would get a chuckle out of it.

"I should have known. It was only a matter of time. But then, he was not obvious or we would have caught on sooner."

Taking her arm, Fargo steered her between two of the freight wagons, saying, "That made no kind of sense."

"It is Cranmeyer," Myrtle said, and sighed. "We reckon he has a thing for Mavis."

"Lust or love?"

"It could be either but I lean to the love. We catch him giving her looks from time to time. When she talks to him, his face lights up like a candle," Myrtle related. "Then when we were loading a wagon for this trip, she bumped against him by accident and he turned as red as a beet."

"Sounds like love to me," Fargo agreed.

"So now he is particular about who we spend our nights with?" Myrtle sighed. "He is in for heartache. We like our nights more than we like our days."

Fargo saw where Cranmeyer's devotion could pose a problem, and mentioned as much.

"We run into his kind a lot," Myrtle said bitterly. "Men who believe they are in love. And since *they* are in love, they expect us to love them back, and they can't understand it when we don't."

"You can't blame them," Fargo said to hold up his end of the conversation. "The three of you are every man's dream."

"What a sweet thing to say!" Myrtle exclaimed, and squeezed his arm. "But that is no excuse for men to act as if they own us. We are not their property. We are not horses or cows or chickens."

"Not all men think of women as hens."

Myrtle made a sound reminiscent of a goose being strangled. "It figures you would say that, you being a man and all. But it shows how little you know. Ask any female and she will tell you that most males think of them as property. The man decides where they will live. The man decides how to spend their money. Hell, sometimes the man even decides what the woman will wear. Women never get to voice an opinion."

"That is harsh," Fargo said.

"Suit yourself. But I am female, and I have lived with things as they are all my life, and hated it."

"Do your sisters feel the same?"

"Of course. Mavis makes excuses for men, saying they can't help being how they are. Cleo laughs about it but if a man dares to boss her around, he will lose skin to her whip."

Fargo glanced at the bullwhip in Myrtle's own hand. "You three never go anywhere without those, do you?"

"No," was her succinct reply.

The ink of night had enfolded them. Overhead sparkled a canopy of stars. From out of the northwest wafted a strong breeze, bringing with it the yip of a coyote. It was answered by another, much nearer. Behind them the wagons were shadowy blocks except where the firelight lit the canvas and beds.

Myrtle breathed deep and said softly, "God, I love it here! I would never move east."

"You don't mind the dangers?" Fargo asked. A lot of

folks liked to be safe and secure when they went to sleep at night.

"Hell, every breath we take might be our last. Why be bothered by trifles?"

Fargo figured they had gone far enough and went to stop but she kept walking and pulled him with her. "Where are we bound for?" he asked. "California?"

"No, silly." Myrtle chuckled. "I just don't want anyone spying on us. It would make me mad and I am not very nice when I am mad."

"Your sisters would give a holler if someone followed us, wouldn't they?"

"They might not notice." Myrtle looked over her shoulder and continued walking. "We won't take the chance."

Fargo let her lead him where she wanted. For all her talk and her bullwhip, she was no different from any other woman when it came to *that*. But they were in Apache country, and the farther they went, the more uneasy he grew. Finally he said, "If we go any farther we will be in the mountains."

"Oh, all right," Myrtle said. Halting, she faced him, her teeth white against the dark. "What did you have in mind?"

"First things first," Fargo said. "Shed the bullwhip."

"I will do better than that, handsome." Stepping back, Myrtle let the whip fall. She drew her pistol and her knife and set them down. Then, as calmly and casually as if she were undressing for bed, she proceeded to strip off her brown shirt and her britches and the rest of her clothes. Each piece, nicely folded, was placed on top of the bullwhip.

Fargo was riveted by her beauty. He had imagined she would be fine but his imagination had not done her justice. Her body was as perfect as her face. The smooth sheen of her neck, the gentle slope of her shoulders, her superb mounds with their delicate arched nipples, her creamy length of thigh. She would take any man's breath away.

Lowering her arms, Myrtle waited, and when he did not move, she asked, "What are you waiting for? A paper invite?"

Fargo hungrily pulled her to him. The contact of his hands and her skin ignited a brush fire. He kissed her, his tongue delving deep, his hands rising to her breasts so he could pinch her nipples. Some women might object to how hard he did it but not Myrtle. She squirmed with pleasure and her body grew warm with carnal need.

When Fargo drew back, she tugged at his buckskin shirt, saying, "If you expect me to be naked and you not to be, you are mistaken." She began prying at his belt buckle. "I want to feel you as much as you like to feel me."

Fargo pushed her hand away and did it himself. A tiny voice at the back of his mind warned it was not wise to strip off his Colt, given where they were, but he silenced the voice with a mental shrug. He set his holster within quick reach. Then he stripped off his shirt, sat on the ground, and began removing his boots and pants.

The whole while, Myrtle stood with her arms folded, watching and grinning. "And men like to complain that women take too long," she teased.

"I would be in you by now if you did not want us skin to skin," Fargo said.

"No, you would not," Myrtle replied. "If I wanted it quick I would tell you." She rubbed her foot along his leg. "Nice and slow is how I like it and nice and slow is how we will be."

"We do not have all night," Fargo said. He was thinking of Cranmeyer, and Jefferson Grind, and the Mimbres Apaches, and God knew who else was out there.

"Do you have somewhere you need to be?" Myrtle ran her foot higher. "Or is it you are scared of the dark?"

"Keep it up," Fargo said, "and I will take you over my knee and spank you until you beg me to stop."

"Promises, promises," Myrtle taunted. "That I would like to see."

By then Fargo had all his clothes off. "In that case," he said, and swung his legs behind hers. Before Myrtle could think to skip aside, he hooked his feet around her ankles and swept her legs out from under her. It brought her down on top of him and he caught her as she fell. Squealing in delight, she sought to push free, but she did not try too hard. In a twinkling he had her on her belly. "You asked for this," he said, and brought his hand down on her fanny with a loud *smack*.

Arching her back, Myrtle dug her fingers into his leg. "Oh, my! Do that again!"

"Happy to oblige." Fargo smacked her other cheek and she wriggled and opened and closed her legs.

"Again! Please, again!"

Grinning, Fargo smacked her bottom so many times, he lost count. She gasped and shivered and tossed her head from side to side, and when, after a while, he stopped and rolled her onto her back, she flung herself at him as if she were attacking him.

Her fingernails raked his shoulders and biceps. She bit his lower lip and then his upper and then nibbled from his chin to his ear and back again. She did not nibble lightly, either.

"Oh, yes," she moaned. "Like that."

Making love to her was like wrestling a mountain lion. She was never still, not for a second. Her hands, and her mouth, were everywhere, and at no time was she what could be called *gentle*. She liked it rough. The rougher, the better.

Fargo felt a drop of wetness trickle down his chin. He touched it and his finger came away deep scarlet at the tip. "You bit me so hard you drew blood," he declared.

Myrtle did not respond. She was too involved with kissing and licking and biting. A fingernail dug deep into his wrist and he almost yelped. Her teeth raked his neck, virtually scraping him raw.

"Damn, woman," Fargo groused. "Slow down." But his request fell on deaf ears.

Suddenly Myrtle gripped him down low, and squeezed, and Fargo nearly cried out.

Her fierce antics were working; she had him hard, good and hard, and raring to bury himself in her. But when Fargo rolled her onto her back and went to part her legs, she sank her teeth into his shoulder and gripped his manhood to where he thought it would rupture. Pushing her back, he snapped, "It isn't a broom handle!"

Lust hooding her eyes, Myrtle Frazier chuckled. "What's wrong? Don't tell me the big, tough man can't take it. Cry if you want. I won't mind."

"Bitch," Fargo said.

Myrtle laughed. "If you want me, you must work for it." She gave his member a yank that he swore nearly tore it off. "Some men can't take it. They are too weak. How about you? I took you for tough but maybe I was mistaken. Maybe you are mush inside."

"Here is your mush," Fargo said, and slamming her onto her back, he pressed her legs wide with his knees, quickly aligned the tip of his throbbing lance with her moist slit, and rammed up into her.

"Ohhhhhhh!" Myrtle bucked like a mustang, nearly heaving him off. "This is how I like it!"

"Good," Fargo said, and gave it to her again. Rarely was he this rough with a woman. Most preferred tamer lovemaking.

Myrtle gripped his shoulders and churned her hips in wild release. "Yes! Yes! Oh, yes!"

Fargo glanced toward the wagons. They were far enough away that no one should hear her, or so he hoped. "Keep it down?"

Bucking in a frenzy, Myrtle tossed her head from side to side. Her back was a bow, her hips rising into the air with each violent thrust.

Fargo had to hand it to her. He had lain with some wildcats in his travels but seldom one as wholeheartedly lustful as she was about sharing herself. As if to demonstrate, she left bloody furrows in his back from his shoulder blades to his hips.

"Do that one more time," Fargo growled. In his estimation she was getting carried away.

"Do you like it, big man?" Myrtle husked. "Does it make you want to throw back your head and howl?"

Holding her down, Fargo drove up into her. The night dissolved into a blur, the wind seemed to have died, the ground did not exist. There was him and there was her and that was all there was. For her part, Myrtle flung her arms around his shoulders and clung to him as if she were drowning and he was a log that would keep her afloat.

"Harder!" Myrtle enthusiastically urged. "I want it harder!"

Fargo did it harder and harder, but she still wasn't satisfied. Sliding her legs over his shoulders, he bent her in half. On each inward thrust he rose onto the tips of his toes, driving into her with all his weight.

"There! That's it!" Myrtle's teeth found his jaw. Her nails clawed his ribs. "What you do, don't stop!"

A vague sense of something not being as it should nipped at Fargo's consciousness. He became aware of the wind on his naked body, of their surroundings, of the dark. Thinking that her outcries had been heard, he shot a quick look toward the freight wagons but saw no one. He was lowering his head to mold his mouth to hers when he happened to glance to the west toward the distant mountains, and the blood in his veins congealed into ice.

Someone was watching them.

Not twenty feet away, motionless as a statue, was the darkling silhouette of a person.

Fargo was so surprised, he almost stopped stroking. But he did not want to let on that he knew they were being watched so he kept driving his member into Myrtle while groping for his gun belt. It had been right next to him. But in the sensual fury of their coupling they had rolled away from it and now he had no idea where it was.

Fargo's unease mounted. The figure might be from the freight train, except that whoever it was had come up on them from the other direction. It could be a local, but locals did not wander around at night alone and on foot. Not if they were fond of living.

The answer hit him with the force of a physical blow.

If it wasn't a mule skinner—

And it wasn't a local—

It must be an Indian.

And if it was an Indian, then it might well be a mortal enemy of the white man; it might well be an Apache.

No sooner did the realization dawn than Fargo heard a sound that confirmed his hunch: the twang of a bow-string.

11

Fargo exploded into the moment the instant the bow twanged. He thought he knew where the Colt was and he flung himself toward it. Myrtle was clinging to him so tightly, her arms and legs clamped fast, that he took her with him, rolling both of them over, not once but several times, and when he did, she cried out. Not from pain or surprise.

She was gushing.

Something pricked Fargo's side. He thrust his arm toward where he hoped to find his holster and frantically ran his hand back and forth but it was not there.

Keenly aware that the next arrow might hit him dead center, Fargo tried to sit up but Myrtle's thrashing hindered him. "Get off!" he urged. But he might as well ask her to get up and dance a waltz. She was lost in the sweet oblivion of release. The sensations between her legs eclipsed all else.

Then his questing fingers bumped something, an object that moved when he brushed it. He clawed with his fingers and snagged his gun belt. In a thrice he had the Colt out and cocked and was twisting toward the silhouette with the bow—only the silhouette was no longer there.

The Indian was gone.

Fargo glanced right and left and then over his shoulder. He cocked the Colt and lay there waiting for Myrtle to spend herself. She had no inkling of what had happened and was impaling herself on his pole again and again and again.

"Oh! Oh! Oh!"

Fargo wished he could quiet her. He might be able to hear the patter of stealthy footfalls or the drum of hooves. But she went on and on until finally she moaned and collapsed, her limbs turning to putty as she oozed into a languid sprawl.

Quickly disentangling himself and rising, Fargo walked in a circle. His main mast was at full sail, as it were, but there was nothing he could do about that. He satisfied himself they were alone, then examined his side. He had been nicked, nothing more. Hurriedly, he donned his buckskins and boots. He was lucky to be alive and did not want to push that luck.

The warrior might return. That he was hostile was proven by the arrow, and his next attempt might succeed if—

The arrow! Fargo cast about for it. It had to be there somewhere, and it was, an arm's length from where Myrtle lay with her limbs spread eagle. Eagerly, he snatched it up.

No two tribes made their arrows exactly alike. By the markings and how it was made he should be able to tell the tribe the warrior was from.

"What in the world are you doing?" Myrtle dreamily asked. She patted the ground. "Lie down next to me and we will cuddle."

Fargo sat next to her and her fingers plucked at his buckskins.

"You are dressed already?" Myrtle said. "Damn. Wasn't I any good for you? Most men would be as limp as wet rags right about now."

"We aren't alone," Fargo said quietly.

"What?" Myrtle rose onto her elbows. "Who did you see? One of Cranmeyer's new guards? None of the mule skinners would be stupid enough to spy on me."

"It wasn't anyone from the freight train." Fargo held the arrow so she could see it.

With an oath, Myrtle was on her hands and knees. Hastily gathering up her clothes, she swiftly slipped into them, saying as she dressed, "I bet it was an Apache. Or maybe a Navajo. They have been acting up lately." She patted her revolver but did not draw it. "One thing for sure. It wasn't a Pima or a Maricopa. To my knowledge they have never harmed a white man and would not want to."

"We will know as soon as I examine this arrow," Fargo predicted.

Back to back, they jogged to the wagons. Fargo did not say anything to anyone but went straight to one of the fires. He held the arrow close to the flames, and disappointment set in. "Damned peculiar," he muttered.

The arrow did not have any markings. Not a single one. From its barbed tip to its feathers it was perfectly plain.

"What do you have there?" a bewhiskered mule skinner asked.

"Nothing," Fargo said, which was exactly right. The arrow was of no use to him. Anyone could have made it. Even a white man.

"Looks like an arrow to me," the mule skinner persisted.

"Where did you get it?" asked another.

One of the guards interjected his two bits. "And why are you carrying it around?"

Myrtle, who was at Fargo's side, said gruffly. "Hush, you infants." She shook her bullwhip for emphasis.

The guard, a younger man who wore two revolvers and had his hat pushed back on his head, snorted. "Who do you think you are, lady, telling us what we should do?"

"You are new or you would not ask," Myrtle said without taking her eyes off the arrow.

"The way you talk," the young guard said.

A driver raised his gaze from the crackling flames. "Leave her be, boy, if you know what is good for you."

"I am not a boy," the young man said testily. "And I will do as I damn well please."

"Then damn well shut your mouth," said another.

Taking a step back, the new man regarded the rest of them with ill-concealed contempt. "What the hell is the matter with all of you? Why do you treat this woman and her sisters as if they are special?"

"They are, Dawson," said the first driver.

"Hell, they are females," Dawson declared derisively.

Myrtle tore her eyes from the arrow and fixed them on him. "What was that supposed to mean?"

"That I am not afraid of you," Dawson boasted. "No man can be afraid of a woman and still call himself a man."

"Is that so?"

"Damn it, boy," snapped yet another. "Be real careful or you will step in it, and there will be nothing we can do."

Dawson laughed. "Listen to yourself. You and the rest of these sheep about wet yourselves whenever any of these stupid women come anywhere near you."

Myrtle slowly straightened. "Did my ears hear what they think they just heard?"

"I stand by what I said," Dawson declared.

"Oh, hell." The first driver stood. "The only one who is stupid here, boy, is you." He and the others stood and began to back away.

"You are cows, all of you," Dawson said to Myrtle. "And cows are not much for brains."

"Cows now, is it?"

By now all the men were up and putting distance between themselves and Dawson.

"What has gotten into you?" Dawson addressed them. "You act as if you are afraid for your lives."

The first driver shook his head. "It is not us who should be afraid, boy. It is you."

"Yellow, the whole bunch," Dawson said in disgust. "And of a woman, no less! A silly, swaggering, overbearing—" He got no further.

Myrtle's bullwhip flicked up and out and the lash wrapped around Dawson's neck. He let out with a startled squawk as he was pulled off balance. Stumbling, he caught himself and clawed at the lash only to have it uncoil at a twist of Myrtle's arm.

"Insult me again."

Dawson was speechless with indignation. Some of the men laughed, which only made him madder. "How dare you!" he finally exploded.

"Haven't you heard?" Myrtle sarcastically asked. "The Frazier girls will dare anything or anyone. We have bark on our trees, which is more than can be said for upstarts like you."

"I warned you," Dawson said, rubbing his throat.

"Save your breath," Myrtle snapped. "I don't scare easy, and I certainly am not afraid of a wet-behind-the-ears sprout like you."

Dawson flushed and lowered his hand to his holster. "One more crack like that and there will be hell to pay, female or no female."

Myrtle uttered a bark of contempt. "Keep my gender out of this. It does not count."

"You should not be here," Dawson dug himself in deeper. "Dealing with Apaches and the like is men's work. If you had any sense, you and your sisters would light a shuck."

"That does it," Myrtle said. Suddenly her bullwhip came alive, arcing through the air and settling around Dawson's wrist. He tried to jerk free but was yanked off balance and fell to his knees.

A few of the other men chuckled or laughed but most recognized the seriousness of the situation. Fargo certainly did but he was not about to stick his nose in. The young fool had brought the tempest down on his own head and now he must weather the storm.

"Damn you, bitch!" Dawson fumed. He pulled on the whip but it was as taut as wire. "Let go of me!"

"Say please," Myrtle said.

"Like hell."

Myrtle tugged on the whip, spilling him onto his hands. "Were you born a jackass or do you work at it?"

"I am not amused," Dawson growled.

"And you think I am?" Myrtle shot back. She let slack into the bullwhip, enough so he could stand. But when he reached to uncoil the whip from his wrist, she took a quick step back, making it taut again. "No, you don't!"

Dawson appealed to the other men. "Are you just going to sit there or do something?"

"Like what, boy?" a driver asked.

"Want us to fetch Cranmeyer and Krupp to come rescue you?" a second asked.

By now Dawson was red from collar to hair. Pivoting toward Myrtle, he loudly declared, "Enough! I have been patient with you, woman, but my patience is at an end. Release me this instant or I will not be to blame for what happens."

Myrtle was not the least bit intimidated. "All you have to do is say you are sorry."

"What?"

"You heard me. Apologize and I will let you go without too many hard feelings."

His fists clenched, shaking from the intensity of his seething emotions, Dawson practically screeched, "*You* took a whip to *me* and you want *me* to say I am sorry to *you*?"

"It is not the whip; it is your manners," Myrtle said. "Be sensible and this will not end badly."

"Oh, it will end, all right," Dawson said. "But it will not end as you expect." With that, he did the last thing he should have done. He stabbed his other hand for his other revolver.

"No!" several voices bellowed.

The young guard did not heed. He had been driven over the brink, and now he was out to punish the person who had humiliated him. In a quick draw he cleared leather, and they all heard the *click* of the hammer being thumbed back.

Myrtle's arm was a blur. She snapped the whip free and slashed it at his other wrist, all in a single, smooth motion, her intent being to stop him before he got off a shot.

But Dawson was not to be caught flat-footed twice.

He sidestepped, his revolver continuing to rise until it was pointed squarely at Myrtle. "Now I have you, you miserable bitch!" he crowed.

Whether he would have squeezed the trigger was impossible to say. He was not given the chance. For even as he spoke, a second bullwhip cracked and wrapped around his wrist even as a third coiled about his neck.

Mavis and Cleopatra had heard the commotion and rushed to help their sister.

"What is going on here?" Cleopatra demanded of Myrtle.

"He is not much for females."

"One of those," Mavis said.

"We should flay him to the bone," Cleopatra proposed. "That should teach him."

Dawson was cussing and struggling mightily to free himself. He still held his revolver, which he waved wildly about as he tugged and jerked and twisted. Maybe he forgot he had the hammer back. Maybe that was why he appeared so shocked when the revolver went off.

"Oh!" Myrtle said.

A crimson stain had blossomed on her shirt, high on her right shoulder. She looked at the wound, then at Dawson. "That was a damn fool thing to do," she said, and collapsed.

Dawson turned to say something. What it was, no one would ever know. For even as he opened his mouth, Cleopatra howled like a she-wolf that had just lost a cub. Her bullwhip cracked as loud as the shot, and the next instant Dawson was screaming with blood streaming from his ruptured right eye. Once again Cleopatra's bullwhip cracked, and everyone saw it slice into Dawson's left eye as neatly as a sharp knife into a grape.

Dawson shrieked and staggered.

Some of the men, Fargo included, started toward him.

From across the camp Cranmeyer hollered, "Hold on, there! What is going on?"

Suddenly Fargo found himself between Cleopatra and Dawson—as the whip described a sizzling arc in his direction.

12

Bullwhips had been around for as long as anyone knew. In Revolutionary War times, and before, they were used to drive stock. Other countries had them. Fargo once talked to a professor who claimed whips had been used by the ancient Greeks and Romans.

Bullwhips came in different sizes and lengths. Those on the frontier tended to be heavier than those in the East. Some whips had wooden stocks; others had leather. Most stocks were weighted with lead. The whip itself could be anywhere from fifteen to twenty-five feet, or more.

Bullwhips were formidable weapons. The snap of a bullwhip was like the crack of a gun, and the whip as fast as a bullet. They could take out an eye, as Cleopatra had just done to Dawson. They could take off an ear. They sliced flesh as easily as a sword. They could even break bones.

Small wonder, then, that as Cleopatra's arm moved, so did Fargo. He threw himself at the ground and the whip passed over his head, missing him by a whisker.

Cleopatra instantly snapped the whip back.

Rolling onto his side, Fargo saw her cock her arm. Cranmeyer shouted something. Then the lash flashed, whizzing over Fargo. He saw it strike, saw Dawson's throat rupture and blood gout in a bright spray.

Blinded, screeching his head off, Dawson clutched at his throat, and staggered. No one moved to help him.

The men were in shock. Myrtle was on the ground. Mavis was smiling.

Cleopatra was not done. She cocked her arm to wield the whip again.

"Enough!"

The command did not come from Cranmeyer. It came from Ezekiel Stack. He stood apart from the rest, his hand close to his holster and his pearl-handled Remington.

"He shot my sister!" Cleo raged.

"You have done enough," Stack said.

Cleo tore her gaze from Dawson, who had pitched to his knees. "Stay out of this, damn you! I do not aim to stop until he is dead."

"You have done enough," Stack repeated.

"To hell with you." Cleopatra swept her arm back and sent the lash snaking toward her victim.

If Fargo had blinked he would have missed Stack's draw. The man was that fast. And accurate, ungodly accurate. His shot severed the lash as neatly as a knife and the severed half fell to earth. It was a marvelous shot. Fargo was not sure even he could have done it.

The tableau froze. Cleo stared at her broken whip in baffled fury. The drivers and guards were astounded.

Only Mavis moved, drawing her arm back with her own bullwhip raised.

Stack spun toward her, his Remington steady in his hand. "Don't," he said quietly.

Mavis froze.

"I could have shot her but I shot her whip," Stack said. "It is over. Tend to Myrtle."

Mavis glanced at her stricken sister and slowly lowered her bullwhip. "It is over," she agreed.

Cleopatra was not as forgiving. "Like hell! Look at what he did!" She shook what was left of her whip. "I will need a whole new lash, thanks to him!"

"Dawson will need a new life," Stack said, and slid the Remington into his holster.

Fargo stood. "That was some shooting," he said by way of praise.

"I should have done it sooner," Stack said. He was staring at Dawson, who was on his belly, convulsing in the final throes of death.

"He brought it on himself," a driver remarked.

"He was young," Stack said. "The young never know any better." He sighed and bowed his head. "I liked the kid. He showed promise."

The rest had come out of their dazes and were flocking around. Krupp took charge, snapping orders like a soldier. Krupp apparently had some experience with wounds and tried to stem the flow of blood, but his effort was too little and much too late.

"Forget him!" Cleopatra snapped. "My sister needs you more than he does."

Krupp glared at her.

Myrtle was in considerable pain but she was holding up well. Mavis and Cleopatra knelt on either side of her and Mavis began cutting away Myrtle's shirt to expose the wound.

Cranmeyer wheeled on them, jabbing a finger at Cleo. "You had no call to do that. You have cost me a guard."

"There are plenty left," was her rejoinder.

"That is not the point," Cranmeyer said sternly. "I have had to warn you before about that temper of yours. This time you have gone too far. I have half a mind to fire you."

"Go right ahead," Cleopatra said. "But remember. When I go, my sisters go with me. You will need to find three mule skinners to take our place."

That gave Cranmeyer pause. They were in the middle of nowhere. The nearest town where he could find men to replace them was Las Cruces, and that would take days.

Cleo was not done. "Any outfit in the territory would be happy to hire us. Jefferson Grind would be particularly pleased."

"You wouldn't," Cranmeyer said.

"We have to eat."

Mavis nodded. "We would rather work for you, Tim.

But if you leave us no choice, we will do what we have to." She motioned at Myrtle. "Now quit all this damn talk and do something about our sister."

Fargo had listened to enough. He reclaimed his tin cup, went to the deserted fire at the other end of camp and filled it to the brim. As he hunkered there, holding the hot cup in his hands, spurs tinkled.

"Mind if I join you?" Stack squatted and filled his own cup. He went to drink, then nodded at the arrow Fargo had set down when pouring. "Are you giving up your Colt for a bow?"

Briefly, Fargo told him about his encounter, ending with, "The arrow is not Apache or any other tribe. It could have been made by a white man, for all I know."

"Or a breed," Stack said.

Fargo looked at him.

"When you do what I do for a living, you are naturally curious about others who do the same," Stack said in his quiet manner. "I have heard about a breed who hires out to kill. He goes by the name of Fraco. He is supposed to be good at what he does."

"And?" Fargo prompted when Stack stopped.

"The last I heard, this Fraco was working for Jefferson Grind." Stack nodded at the arrow again. "And this Fraco is partial to a bow over a gun."

Fargo mulled the information and concluded, "It could be Grind sent him to find out what happened to Wilson and Becker and those other two."

"Could be," Stack agreed.

"It could be Fraco spotted our camp and was prowling around and took it on himself to give Cranmeyer a scare by killing me."

"That sounds like something the breed would do," Stack agreed.

"If he had a horse, he will leave tracks. In the morning I will look for them." Fargo might be able to trail Fraco back to Grind and put an end to the feud before the freight train reached the mountains.

"If you don't mind some company, I will go with you," Stack offered.

Fargo was inclined to say no. He liked to work alone. But if Wilson had told the truth and Grind still had eleven men with him, it would be smart to trim the odds. "We head out at first light."

"I will be ready."

Fargo rose, taking his coffee with him. He found Cranmeyer among a group watching Krupp tend to Myrtle. Cleopatra and Mavis hovered like mother hawks, not letting any of the men come too close. Fargo informed Cranmeyer of his plan.

Krupp overheard, and glanced up from winding a bandage. "Stack thinks it was Fraco who tried to get you with that arrow?"

"Have you heard of him?" Cranmeyer asked.

"I have seen him," Krupp said.

"How did he impress you?"

"Mean as a stuck snake," Krupp said. "He is not all that big and not all that scary-looking but there is something about him that makes you think he would slit your throat and not bat an eye."

"One of those," Cranmeyer said.

Krupp had more to impart. "He is more Injun than white. His hair, his skin, you would think he was Navajo or some such. Then you see his eyes. Gray as fog and as cold as ice."

Fargo had a question. "How many has he killed?"

"No one knows. For years he lived off up in the mountains. Some say with the Apaches. Others say he was with the Navajos. Rumor has it he went on raids with them and killed his share of whites." Krupp paused. "A few years ago he began offering his talents for money, and has been hiring out ever since."

"And now he works for my bitterest enemy," Cranmeyer said. "It figures Grind would hire him. The man has few scruples."

"Fraco has even less," Krupp said. "They say he can

kill a man in a hundred ways. Men, women, even kids, it makes no difference to him so long as he is paid."

"I am surprised the army has not gotten hold of him by now," Cranmeyer commented.

Krupp looked away. "It is not for a lack of trying on their part."

Fargo wasn't surprised. While it was true renegades were routinely hunted down, the army was more concerned about organized bands. Lone wolves like Fraco were low in priority.

Cranmeyer turned to him. "You would be doing the territory a tremendous favor if you were to give this Fraco his due."

"So you don't mind if Stack and me head out after him?"

"Not at all. We will get by. I will ride point myself."

"With me at your side," Krupp said.

Clapping him on the back, Cranmeyer said fondly, "Would that all those who work for me were as devoted as you."

Extra guards were posted, one at each point of the compass. Instead of a single nighthawk, Krupp assigned three. He was taking no chances on the mules being driven off or stolen. Without them, the wagons were so many dead turtles.

It was shortly after midnight when Fargo turned in. First he picketed the Ovaro. Then he spread his blankets, propped his saddle as a pillow and lay on his back with his hands folded on his chest. Soon he was on the verge of drifting off. The slight scrape of a sole brought him back to the world of the real. He pushed up, the Colt springing into his hand as if it were part of him.

"I didn't mean to spook you," Cleopatra Frazier said.

Fargo let down the Colt's hammer. "Shouldn't you be with your sisters?" Myrtle was bundled in blankets over by a wagon, and Mavis was watching over her.

Cleopatra put a hand on his arm. In the starlight she was incredibly beautiful. "I don't want any hard feelings between us."

"Why would there be?" Fargo asked, knowing the answer but wanting her to say it.

"Some of the men are mad at me over Dawson."

"Can you blame them?"

Cleo's eyes flashed. "Can you blame *me*? He shot my sister. Maybe I lost my head but I had cause."

"There is no maybe about it," Fargo said.

"You keep missing the point. He *shot* her."

"By accident. I was there. I saw the whole thing."

"And you are mad at me like all the rest."

"I am not in love with you," Fargo said.

"I was afraid you would feel this way."

"Go away. I need sleep." Fargo turned back toward his blankets but she held on to his arm.

"I don't want you upset. I would like to go on being friends."

"What does it matter?" Fargo was being hard on her but she had it coming. "You and your sisters get by just fine by yourselves."

"We are women," Cleopatra said.

"And my horse is a horse and an owl is an owl," Fargo said. "What does being female have to do with what you did to Dawson?"

"I am not talking about him. I have moved on and am talking about you." Cleo ran her other hand through her copper hair. "When I say we are women, I mean we are no different than any other female."

"Most females don't go around blinding men with bullwhips."

"Please stop. I accept I was hasty. I will send some money to his kin back East to atone."

"How much is his life worth, do you think?"

"Fifty dollars should be enough," Cleo said. "The important thing is that I still get to have my turn."

"Turn?" Fargo said, momentarily confused.

"You know."

"Know what?"

"With you." Cleo grinned and winked.

All Fargo could do was stare.

"Don't look at me like that. Myrtle says you are the best thing in pants she has ever come across. That is saying a lot. Now Mavis and me want to find out for ourselves. I came over to tell you we will abide by our promise if you are still of a mind to have us."

Fargo shook off his amazement. Killing Dawson meant no more to her than squashing a fly. "Is that *all* you think of?"

"There is no rush. It will take us ten days or better to reach Silver Lode. Any night you want me, you have only to say the word and I am yours." Cleo patted his hand, stood and walked off.

"I'll be damned," Skye Fargo said.

13

White men, as a general rule, rode shod horses. Indians, as a general rule, did not.

The tracks that Fargo found shortly after daybreak the next morning were of a horse that was not. Krupp had mentioned that Fraco was more Indian than white, and here was proof.

Stack rode with his hand on his pearl-handled Remington and was his usual taciturn self until about midmorning when he observed, "Fraco does not appear to be in much of a hurry."

Fargo agreed. The tracks showed that the half-breed had held his horse to a walk. They were doing the same, at his insistence. It would not do to come on the killer unexpectedly.

"You would think he'd want to let Grind know as soon as possible that he found us," Stack mentioned.

"He has plenty of time. The wagons are as slow as molasses," Fargo said. "Or it could be that Grind is closer than we think and Fraco does not have far to go."

But his guess proved wrong. Noon came and went, and no Fraco. The afternoon waxed and waned, and no Fraco. They stopped to rest their mounts twice. The second time, foothills lined the horizon.

"He is making for the mountains," Stack said while mopping his brow with his sleeve. "We will not catch up before nightfall."

"We will keep on after dark," Fargo informed him,

and began to undo his bandanna to wipe his face. The heat was blistering.

"You have something in mind, I take it?"

"We have stayed far enough back that he has no idea he is being followed," Fargo said. "He will feel safe in making a fire." And even a small one, at night, was a beacon that could be seen for miles.

"Maybe he will make a cold camp," Stack said. "Or make his camp in a wash or a hollow."

"We should still be able to find him," Fargo said confidently.

"Then what? If he is as vicious as everyone says, trying to take him alive might end with us dead."

"Who said anything about alive?" Fargo rejoined. "He tried to put an arrow into me."

Sunset saw them winding into the arid hills. Fargo was in the lead, as he had been all day, his gaze glued to the ground, and the tracks.

"The Mimbres massacred a settler and his family in these hills just last month," Stack commented.

Fargo knew what Stack was really saying; the farther they went, the greater the risk of encountering Apaches. "They do not stick in any one area too long."

"Let's hope they are elsewhere by now."

Fargo grunted. Apaches on a raid were always on the move, as much to confound pursuers as to hunt for prey.

Twilight descended, transforming the brown of the earth and the rocks and boulders into shades of somber gray. A few clouds scuttled in from the west but Fargo did not foresee a change in the weather. He wound along the base of hill after hill until he came to one that was higher than the rest, and climbed to the crown. He took his time. The Ovaro was tired.

To the west a few lingering streaks of pink decorated the sky but they were fast fading. To the east the black of night was crawling across the land.

Fargo leaned on his saddle horn and waited.

Stack looked at him quizzically but did not say anything.

Gradually the entire sky darkened. Stars sprinkled the vault above. Out of the northwest came a brisk wind. In the far distance a mountain lion shrieked.

Fargo scoured the foothills and the looming mass that betokened the mountains beyond. He might as well be peering into the depths of a well. There was not a glimmer of light anywhere.

"I told you," Stack broke their long silence. "Fraco is too savvy to make a fire that can be seen."

No sooner were the words out of his mouth than a pinpoint of orange appeared amid the black.

"There," Fargo said, and pointed.

"Fraco is getting careless, I reckon."

They made for the speck. Fargo picked his way with care, as much as for the welfare of their mounts as to ensure Fraco did not hear them coming. He drew rein often to listen. Several times they lost sight of the orange but it always reappeared.

Fargo's nerves jangled at every sound. This was not like sneaking up on an outlaw. Most white men had the eyes and ears of a tree stump and were easily taken once they bedded down for the night. Indians, and half-breeds who were more Indian than white, were different. They had the senses of a wild animal. Their hearing was acute, their eyesight sharp. Taking them unawares was next to impossible.

The orange glow, as it turned out, was on the slope of the first mountain, a third of the way up the slope. It had grown in size from a speck to fingers of flame.

"From here we go on foot." Fargo shucked the Henry from the saddle scabbard and swung down.

The slope was steep, their footing at times made treacherous by loose rocks and soil. Fargo was glad when they stumbled on a gully that split the mountain like a scar. They could follow it toward the campfire.

Coyotes were in full chorus. Once something snorted and ran off, the clatter of small hooves hinting it was a deer.

Fargo was impressed by Stack. Unlike a lot of whites,

who blundered around in the dark like blind bulls in a china shop, Stack was almost as quiet as he was.

The gully's many twists and turns prevented Fargo from keeping the campfire in sight. He noticed that the glow had grown even more, and that troubled him. Indians usually kindled small fires to avoid discovery. Whites favored big fires, the better to keep warm and keep the dark at bay. This fire was proving to be bigger than any warrior with a shred of self-preservation would ever make.

Stack noticed, too, and when the fire was only a few hundred yards above them, he whispered, "If that is Fraco, I am a schoolmarm."

They continued to climb anyway and soon were near enough to see that two figures were next to the fire and several horses were tethered nearby. The pair were whites, as Fargo expected. But what he did not expect was that one of them would have waist-length brunette hair framing a baby-smooth face that could not have seen twenty years. The man she was with did not appear old enough to shave.

"Oh, hell," Stack said.

Cupping a hand to his mouth, Fargo hollered, "Hallo the camp! We would like to come in!"

The stripling leaped to his feet, fumbling with a rifle. As he leveled it the woman darted behind him and peeked out past his shoulder.

"Who are you? What do you want?" her protector challenged in a tone thick with poorly disguised fear.

"We are friendly," Fargo said. "We will come in with our hands empty if you will promise not to shoot." Fright made for twitchy trigger fingers.

The young woman whispered something and the stripling nodded. "All right! But keep your hands where I can see them!"

Fargo set the Henry down and nodded at Stack, who reluctantly put down his rifle.

"Here we come! Go easy on that trigger!"

Arms well out from his sides, Fargo climbed into the

circle of firelight. Stack came with him, and Stack did not look happy.

"That is far enough!" The stripling wagged his rifle for emphasis. "What is it you want?"

Fargo did not mince words. "What the hell are you doing here?" he gruffly demanded.

The brunette gasped and her peach-fuzz defender hardened with anger.

"I will thank you not to use that kind of language in front of my wife. And why we are here is none of your affair."

"Listen to me, boy," Fargo said. "These are the Mimbres Mountains. They get their name from the Mimbres Apaches, who think the only good white is a dead white. And they don't give a hoot if the white is male or female."

"Watch your tongue, sir," the stripling snapped. "Reckless talk like that will scare Harriet."

The brunette tugged at her husband's sleeve and said, "That is all right, Howard. I think he is just warning us to be careful."

"Howard and Harriet?" Stack said, and laughed.

"Here now," Howard said, his anger tempered by puzzlement. "What strikes your funny bone?"

Stack minced even fewer words than Fargo did. "You are a damned fool, boy, to bring that girl up here. You are a worse fool for being by yourselves and not with a wagon train."

"I have this," Howard said, extending his rifle. "And I will keep the fire going all night to keep any hostiles at bay."

"I take it back, boy," Stack said. "You are worse than a fool. You are a jackass." Lowering his arms, he wheeled and said to Fargo, "You can try and talk some sense into them if you want. I will fetch the horses. I did not like leaving them untended."

"Hold on, there!" Howard commanded, but Stack strode into the dark and was gone.

"That was unspeakably rude," Harriet said.

Fargo came to Stack's defense, saying, "He was trying to get you to understand. You are in *Apache* country."

"As if we don't know that," Howard said. "But we have come all the way from Santa Fe without spotting a single redskin."

"You won't see any until they are ready to be seen," Fargo said.

"Oh, please. You sound like that old man in Santa Fe who warned us not to come."

"Why didn't you listen?"

"To what? His tall tales about Apaches being able to move about like ghosts? To his claim that they can run all day and not tire, or hide so well they are invisible?" Howard shook his head. "I stopped believing in ogres when I was six."

Harriet threw in, "We have read about the big strikes up to Silver Lode and we aim to have a claim of our own."

"All the silver ore in the world is not worth your lives."

"I wish you would stop," Howard said. "In a week or so we will reach Silver Lode and everything will be fine."

Harriet nodded enthusiastically. "They say that Silver Lode will be as big as New Orleans in no time."

"Oh, hell," Fargo said. People said that about most every new camp and the people were nearly always wrong. Most strikes petered out within a year and the camps and towns they gave birth to withered and died.

Stepping from behind her husband, Harriet said, "It is kind of you to be so concerned. But I have complete confidence in Howard. The Apaches do not worry me."

"They are not the only ones you have to watch out for. There is a killer on the loose, a renegade called Fraco. If he spots your fire he will treat you to more than a warning."

"He doesn't scare me," Howard boasted.

"You wouldn't stand a prayer, boy."

"I am a man, thank you."

Fargo tried one last time. "I am with a freight train

bound for Silver Lode. Why not join up with us? It will take you longer to get there but you will be safer."

"No, thanks," Howard said.

Fargo looked at Harriet.

"No, thank you. The sooner we reach Silver Lode, the sooner we can afford all the things I want to buy."

She made it sound as if striking it rich was as easy as lacing a boot.

Fargo touched his hat brim. "I have said my piece. Good luck to you." They would need it.

He retrieved the Henry and started down. There was no reasoning with some folks. Those two thought they knew it all and had an answer for everything. Experience could teach them how ignorant they were, and sometimes that experience came at great cost.

With a shake of his head Fargo dismissed them from his mind. He must stay alert or he might be the one learning a lesson.

The night had gone quiet. The wind was still. Fargo had the illusion he was walking through a great emptiness and that he was the only living thing in all the void.

He had descended about three hundred feet when a scream shattered the illusion, a scream of mortal terror torn from a female throat. It was followed by the blast of a rifle.

Fargo whirled.

Another scream rose to the high peaks, a cry that Fargo would remember on dark and lonely nights. It was all the fear in the human soul given substance in sound. It was the height of pure fright and the depths of darkest despair.

His legs churning, Fargo flew toward the campfire. He hoped against hope he would not find what he was bound to find, and mentally cursed all fools and know-it-alls.

The fire still crackled. The flames still blazed bright. They revealed that the horses were still there. And so was a body, sprawled in a grotesque mockery of the life that once animated it.

Howard was on his back in the center of a spreading

101

crimson pool. His throat had been slit. Slit so violently, and so deeply, his head was attached by a few shreds of skin.

Fargo looked for sign of the wife but she was nowhere to be seen. "Harriet?" he shouted.

The answer came in the form of another scream from somewhere above.

14

Fargo swore, and flew on up the slope. Some men would not have gone to her rescue. Some would have said that she and her fool of a husband brought their fate down on their own heads. Some would not have gone because their spines were tinged yellow.

Fargo was no coward. As for foolishness, he had done a few things over the years that made him question whether he had a lick of common sense. But the real reason Fargo went bounding up that slope to save a woman whose last name he did not even know was that he suspected the party responsible for slaying her husband and abducting her was the man he was after.

It could be Apaches. But Apaches usually holed up at night.

Odds were, it was Fraco.

The dark was a soup of shadow and menace. Fargo stayed alert for boulders and anything else he might collide with. Soon he was in among a scattering of evergreen shrubs.

The screaming had stopped. Fargo was about to yell Harriet's name when he suddenly drew up short.

Talk about foolish! Here he was, barreling through the night with no thought to his own welfare. It could be just what Fraco wanted. The woman might be a lure to draw him into an ambush.

Fargo broke out in a sweat. Another mistake like that could get him killed. He firmed his grip on the Henry and stalked forward cautiously, pausing often to test his surroundings for signs of life.

Seconds dragged on millstones of unease. His nerves were stretched to the point that a *scritch*ing sound brought him around in a crouch with his trigger finger starting to tighten, but it was only a small animal of some kind that went scrabbling off in fear.

Fargo swallowed. He was letting Fraco's reputation spook him. He must remember that he had fought Indians more times than most ten men combined. If anyone was a match for the half-breed, it was him.

Still, the expectation of getting an arrow in the back was enough to make any man cautious. Fargo chafed at his slow hunt but it could not be helped. To move any faster invited disaster.

He could not say how long he had been at it when hooves thudded behind him. Crouching, he waited, and soon a rider appeared leading a black-and-white horse by the reins. "Over here!" he said, but not too loudly, and showed himself.

"Finally," Stack said, drawing rein. "I have been looking all over for you."

"How did you know which way I had gone?"

"I heard the woman scream. I was still a ways from their camp, and when I got there and found you missing, I figured you had gone after her." Stack's tone suggested he did not think it wise.

"I think Fraco has her," Fargo said, stepping to the Ovaro. "He could be anywhere."

"Then why in hell are you doing this? You don't owe her or her idiot of a husband anything."

"You keep forgetting that Fraco tried to put an arrow in me."

Stack leaped to the obvious conclusion. "And you are hankering to blow out his wick. That I can understand. Any man who won't stand up for himself is not much of a man."

"You don't have to help if you don't want to," Fargo told him.

Stack was silent a bit; then he said, "I am no Samaritan. And I have no grudge with Fraco. But we are on the same side in this and I will stand by you, come what may."

Fargo gigged the Ovaro. They made better targets on horseback, but by the same token they were higher off the ground and could see farther. Then there was another factor—Fargo had learned to rely on the Ovaro's hearing and sense of smell. He had lost count of the number of times the stallion had saved his skin with a timely warning.

They roved for a good half hour but did not turn up a trace of their quarry or his captive.

Reining up, Fargo said in disgust, "We are wasting our time. They could be anywhere."

"They say the breed is fond of dainty morsels," Stack remarked.

Fargo scowled. It would be a horrible way to die, the deepest fear of many a female. "We will go back to their camp and wait until dawn."

"Why bother? The dunce of a husband is dead."

"They had three horses," Fargo reminded him. The horses had been picketed, and if they could not pull loose they would starve. He brought the Ovaro around and headed down the mountain.

Stack came up alongside him. For some reason he was being talkative. "What do you aim to do with their horses?"

"I haven't given it any thought," Fargo said. Beyond ensuring they didn't suffer.

"By rights they are ours now," Stack said. "We could hold on to them until we get to Silver Lode and sell them for three times what we would get for them in Las Cruces or Albuquerque."

"I had no idea you are so fond of money."

"I hire out my pistol to those who can afford me, don't I?" Stack justified his mercenary streak by adding, "A man has to eat."

"Some money is easier on the conscience than others," Fargo noted.

"I am not fussy in that regard. Once I accept a job, I do what needs to be done and I do not cry about it after."

Food for Fargo's thoughts. When he got right down to it, there wasn't much difference between Stack and Fraco. Both were killers. Both hired out their talents for top dollar. That one was white and the other only half was of no consequence whatsoever. It wasn't the color of a man's skin that made him who he was. It was the man under that skin.

The fire had shrunk but was still crackling. Fargo stripped the Ovaro and spread out his blankets. He was bone weary but before turning in he went through the personal effects of the recently departed Howard and his missing wife, Harriet. Half a dozen packs were crammed with provisions and clothes. Most of the clothes were Harriet's. She had more dresses than a dress shop.

Stack was by the fire, poking it with a stick. "We can sell that stuff, too," he said.

"We could scalp Howard and say we took it off of an Apache and sell it in Silver Lode," Fargo suggested. Scalps sometimes fetched fifty dollars or more.

"That is a good idea."

"I wasn't serious."

"I still think it was a good idea."

Fargo was seeing a whole new side to the man, and he was not liking a lot of what he was seeing. "When this job is over, what then?"

About to jab the stick, Stack glanced over. "I will go on doing what I do. So long as there is money to be paid for pulling the trigger, I will pull it."

"That is all you ever want?"

Stack shrugged. "We are what we are."

"Tell me. Did Cranmeyer hire you to protect him and his wagons, or for another reason?"

"I am not a protector," Stack said.

There Fargo had it. Timothy P. Cranmeyer was not the victim of circumstance he pretended to be. Grind and

Cranmeyer had both hired killers—only Grind hired more.

As if Stack could read his thoughts, he said, "Don't think poorly of Cranmeyer. He is in over his head."

Fargo began rolling up one of his blankets lengthwise. He placed it so one end was on his saddle, then draped another blanket over it. For extra effect he placed his saddlebags about where a man's head would be and placed his hat on his saddlebags.

Stack watched with interest. "Are you expecting Fraco to pay us a visit in the middle of the night?"

"We can't put anything past him," Fargo said. The breed was deadly and devious, and would kill them any way he could. Satisfied with the ruse, he took the Henry and retreated into the dark a stone's throw from the fire.

Stack arranged his blankets similarly and moved off in the opposite direction.

Finding a boulder to sit against, Fargo placed his rifle across his legs. Now all he could do was wait. He stayed awake as long as he could. Eventually his eyelids grew leaden, his chin dipped and he drifted off. He did not sleep well.

In the stillness before dawn, a nicker from the Ovaro snapped Fargo's head up. He scanned the vicinity and cocked his head to the wind but saw and heard nothing. The stallion had its ears pricked toward the slope above them, but after a while it lowered its head and dozed.

Fargo did the same.

The next sound that awakened him was the screech of a jay. To the east the sky had paled, a harbinger of the new day. Fargo stretched and yawned, his stiff muscles protesting. Rising, he surveyed the mountainside. All was peaceful.

Fargo leaned against the boulder until half the stars were erased by the glare of the golden crown on the rim of the world. Kicking his legs to get the kinks out, he crossed to the fire. It took only a minute to rekindle the embers and fan them to flame with puffs of breath.

Enough coffee was in the pot that he did not need to make more.

Stack came out of the scrub. "That was about as comfortable as sleeping on a cactus."

"As soon as the sun is up, we will bury the husband and rejoin Cranmeyer," Fargo proposed.

"Coyotes and buzzards have to eat, too," Stack said.

"I will do it myself if need be." Fargo went to reach for his tin cup and happened to set eyes on his blankets and saddle. For a few moments he was riveted in consternation, unable to understand why the blanket he had rolled up and covered was now on the other side of the saddle. "What the hell?"

"Aren't those your saddlebags?" Stack asked, pointing.

Fargo looked, and suddenly his bewilderment took on darker hues of suspicion and dread. His saddlebags were a dozen feet away. Then it hit him. If the rolled-up blanket was not under the other blanket, why was there a bulge as if a body were underneath?

Stack was apparently wondering the same thing. "It can't be," he said. "No one could have snuck in and out that quiet."

Gripping the edge of the spread blanket, Fargo steeled himself. He had a pretty fair notion of what he would find. Or, rather, whom. He pulled the blanket off and could not resist a gasp.

Stack swore.

Harriet was on her back. She was stark naked. In life she had been pretty but there was nothing pretty about the way she looked now.

Stack said a strange thing. "I can never get used to this. No matter how many times I see it, I just can't."

Harriet's eyes had been gouged out. Her ears had been cut off. Where her nose had been was a jagged cavity. She no longer had breasts. And that was not all. She had been cut, a wound so deep, only a bowie or some other large knife could have made it. The cut started at her pubic region and went clear up and under her ribs.

"Why would he do that?" Stack asked, more to himself than to Fargo.

Fargo shook his head.

The cut was gruesome enough, but what Fraco had done after he cut her was worse. The breed had pulled out her internal organs. Her intestines, her stomach, everything, were gone.

Fargo's own stomach churned but he held the contents down.

"I bet she was alive when he started in on her," Stack said. "They say he loves to torture more than anything."

Fargo could imagine the torment and terror the woman had gone through. Right up to the very end she must have suffered abominably. He spread the blanket back over her and carefully wrapped her in it.

"I don't savvy," Stack said.

Fargo was trying to shake the image from his mind but it was too fresh, too vivid. "Don't savvy what?"

"The breed. He snuck in here right under our noses and placed her under your blanket when he could just as easily have finished us off." Stack scratched his chin. "Why did he let us live?"

Nodding at the figure in the blanket, Fargo said, "Maybe this was his idea of a joke. Maybe he was rubbing our noses in it, showing us how much better than us he is. Or maybe this was his way of daring us to keep after him." Or maybe it was for all those reasons, or none of them.

"He must not know who we are," Stack said. "He must think we are settlers or townsfolk."

Fargo doubted whether that would matter.

"I would be insulted if he did," Stack rambled on. "It would mean he has no more respect for us than I do for a bug."

"You are taking this personal."

"I never take anything personal," Stack assured him. "In my line of work that buys an early grave." His eyes narrowed. "But you are, aren't you?"

Yes, Fargo was. The half-breed had put the woman under *his* blanket. It was the same as a drunk throwing whiskey in his face, or a cardplayer calling him a cheat. He would not stand for those insults. He would not stand for this. Sliding his arms under the body, he lifted and carried her to a flat area wide enough for both bodies. He did not have a shovel but he remembered seeing tools in their packs.

Stack did not help dig. He stood with his rifle cradled, scanning the slopes above. "In case he tries to pick us off."

"Didn't you say he is partial to a bow?"

"Howard's rifle is missing."

Sweat was streaming down Fargo's sides. He stopped to press a sleeve to his face.

"We will run into the breed again," Stack predicted. "I feel it in my bones."

Fargo grimly placed his hand on his Colt. He hoped so. And the next time, only one of them would ride away.

15

For three days the freight wagons climbed ever higher into the rugged vastness of the Mimbres Mountains. The rutted excuse for a road twisted and turned like a snake crawling through briars.

Unease gripped the drivers and guards. They were in the heart of Mimbres country now, and the Mimbres were ruthless in their efforts to drive the white invaders out. Every outrider had a hand on a revolver at all times. Every wagon guard kept his rifle handy in his lap. The drivers stayed vigilant and cast many an anxious glance at the slopes to either side and at strips of forest and clusters of boulders that might hide a steely-eyed warrior.

As if the Apaches were not enough of a worry, there was Jefferson Grind and his men. They might strike at any time.

"I am surprised he hasn't already," Timothy P. Cranmeyer remarked the morning of their fourth day in the mountains.

"Maybe losing those men he sent to find you has made him cautious," Fargo speculated.

"Or maybe he has some nasty trick up his sleeve," Krupp said. "He is a devil, that one."

Fargo remembered Wilson saying almost the exact same thing right before he died.

Stack came riding up from the rear of the line. "No sign of anyone trailing us," he reported.

"The men are jumping at shadows," Cranmeyer said.

"If something doesn't happen soon, they will be nervous ruins."

"I will keep them in line, sir," Krupp pledged.

Cranmeyer stared off up the road. "I want one of you to ride on ahead and search for a spot to rest at midday."

"I'll do it," Fargo said. He would rather be on his own anyway. To Stack he said, "Keep an eye on things."

"You can count on me."

Fargo gigged the Ovaro and soon was around a bend and out of sight. He rode alertly, his hand on the Colt. In Apache country a man must never let down his guard. An instant's lapse was all it took to send him into oblivion.

The day was ungodly hot, as all their days had been. Hot and dry and still. Unusually still, Fargo thought. A feeling came over him, a feeling he'd had several times in the past couple of days, that unseen eyes were watching. Nerves, he told himself, without much conviction.

The clomp of the Ovaro's heavy hooves seemed unnaturally loud. More nerves, Fargo thought. He came to another bend and once around it rose in the stirrups.

In the distance reared ever-higher peaks. Silver Lode was up there, with a promise of safety, and whiskey.

Beads of sweat trickled down Fargo's neck and back. To breathe the scorching air was like breathing fire. He was tempted to use his canteen but he refrained. It would be two days before they reached the next water. There might be some closer, but if so, only the Apaches knew where. That was their edge over the white man. They knew every secret spring and tank. Where the whites had to stick to established routes between water holes, the Apaches could roam at will, relying on their secret knowledge to sustain them. Even Apaches needed water now and then.

Lost in his musing, Fargo rounded another twisting turn and idly swiped at particles of dust hanging in the air. Suddenly he stiffened. Dust did not rise into the air on its own accord. It took wind—and there was none at

112

the moment—or else someone had gone by that very spot not five minutes before him.

It could be a white man, or more than one, heading for Silver Lode. Or it could have more sinister meaning. Fargo decided to find out. A light jab of his spurs brought the Ovaro to a trot. The grade grew steep, and he hunched forward in the saddle.

It saved his life.

A rifle cracked and lead nearly took off his left ear. Instantly, he swung onto the stallion's side, hanging by a forearm and a leg, Comanche-style. He half feared the ambusher would shoot the Ovaro but he made it to an outcropping of boulders and drew rein in their shadow.

Involuntarily, Fargo shuddered. It had been close. Half an inch to the right, and he would be lying in the road with a bullet hole in his head.

Shucking the Henry, he levered a round into the chamber. As best he could tell, the shot had come from ahead and to the left of the road. He sought some sign of the shooter but the emptiness mocked him.

Fargo waited. He was in no hurry to ride on. The bushwhacker might still be up there, waiting for another chance.

A lizard scuttled out from under a boulder, saw him and promptly scuttled back under it again.

A hawk soared high in the sky, wings outspread. It wheeled over the slope Fargo suspected harbored the bushwhacker and turned in slow circles, as hunting hawks were prone to do. It showed no alarm.

Apparently the bushwhacker was gone.

Fargo rode on, the Henry across his saddle, and for a half mile or so his skin crawled with the expectation of another shot. But none came. The tension was beginning to drain from him when he came to a broad shelf that would do for their nooning, and drew rein.

Dismounting, Fargo moved to where he could look back down the road. The wagons were not in sight but they should be soon. He squatted and idly plucked at brown blades of grass.

Except for the attempt on his life, the past three days had been uneventful. From dawn until dusk the train was on the move. At night everyone was too tired to do much more than eat and turn in.

The Frazier sisters were keeping to themselves. He had not had a chance to talk to them, let alone go for another stroll. Twice, though, he had noticed Cleopatra eyeing him as if she was hungry and he was food. Which was fine by him. He did not approve of what she had done but he would not refuse her when the time came.

Fargo chuckled. His fondness for women might one day be the death of him. How many times had he ended up in trouble because of them? He had lost count.

Presently the wagons appeared, so far down the mountain the riders were ants. It would be a while before they got there.

Fargo debated riding on and decided to stay put. The Ovaro was tired, and there was no sense in pushing the stallion more than he had to. Horses could be felled by too much heat and not enough water, the same as the people who rode them.

With that in mind, Fargo walked to his saddle and unslung his canteen. He permitted himself several sips. Then, untying and moistening his bandanna, he cooled the stallion.

A fly buzzed past. Fargo was about to retie his bandanna around his neck when the bright gleam of sunlight on metal compelled him to dive flat. He felt slightly foolish in that the flash could be from a vein of quartz or something else.

The boom of a rifle proved otherwise.

In a twinkling Fargo was in motion. Rolling up into a crouch, he threw himself at his saddle and mounted in a single, smooth movement. Even as he used his spurs he was shoving the Henry into the scabbard. He wanted dearly to ride toward the shooter but worry sent him on up the road. Worry not for himself, but for the Ovaro. Apaches liked horse meat as much as whites liked venison, if not more.

Another shot kicked up dirt next to the stallion.

Fargo got out of there. He started to swing onto the Ovaro's side but the stallion veered to avoid a boulder, and the next thing he knew, he was hanging by one ankle and clutching the saddle horn to keep from plunging headfirst to the dirt.

A laugh floated down from above, a short, savage bark of mirth.

Fraco.

Fargo had to do something. He could not keep counting on providence and flight. Accordingly, as soon as he was around the next bend, he swung up and brought the stallion to a stop.

A tug on the Henry and he hit the ground running.

Fargo was taking another gamble. He was going after the breed. If he was wrong, and it wasn't Fraco but a Mimbres war party, he might pay for his mistake with his life.

He sprinted toward the spot where the shot came from, weaving like a wild man in case the shooter had spotted him.

No thunder pealed.

No hot lead sought his flesh.

Fargo was two hundred feet above the road when he heard the beat of hooves. The sound did not come from the road but from the next slope. He pushed himself, running flat out, and spied rising tendrils of dust. He also glimpsed a horse and rider as a gully or a wash was swallowing them.

Out of frustration Fargo kept running. He was praying for a shot, just one clear shot. But he did not see the rider again.

Puffing for breath in the terrible heat, his shirt caked to his body with sweat, Fargo stopped and gulped breaths. All his hard effort had been for nothing.

He was about where the shooter had been when the shot rang out and he glanced about, not really expecting to find anything other than a smudge or two.

To his surprise, there were moccasin tracks. The killer

had made no attempt to hide them. He saw where the man had knelt to shoot. He saw something else, too—something that caught his breath in his throat and sent an icy chill rippling up and down his spine.

"It can't be," Fargo said out loud.

But it was.

In the dirt near the imprint of the killer's knees was a human finger. It had been cut off at the third joint. Bone poked from the pink flesh at the severed end, and a drop of dry blood sprinkled the skin.

Revulsion gripped Fargo. He had seen worse, a lot worse, but this was so unforeseen, it shook him. Hunkering, he poked the finger with the Henry, rolling it over. The person who lost the finger had been white. The dirt under the fingernail suggested it was a white man and not a white woman; women tended to keep their nails cleaner than men.

Fargo straightened. He was not about to touch the damn thing. He turned to return to the Ovaro, and received a second jolt.

Another finger lay a few yards away, in the direction the bushwhacker had taken to reach his mount.

Fargo walked to the second finger. It was the same as the first, only bigger. The middle finger, he reckoned. He went a few yards farther on and there was a third. The little finger this time, right next to a clear set of moccasin prints.

"Fraco, you son of a bitch," Fargo growled. As if there was any doubt who was responsible. But who had lost the fingers? Howard and Harriet had all of theirs.

Wheeling, he retraced his steps.

Soon he was in the saddle again. He passed the spot where he had been shot at and continued on down the mountain to meet the freight wagons.

Cranmeyer, Krupp and Stack were riding point. All three were somber as they drew rein to await him.

"Let me guess," Fargo said before they could get a word out. "Someone is missing."

"A guard," Cranmeyer confirmed. "He was at the

rear. He disappeared just a short while after you rode off. We couldn't find a trace of him anywhere. The Mimbres, I suspect."

"It was Fraco."

"How do you know?" Krupp asked.

Fargo told them about his latest clash with the half-breed. "The fingers I found must belong to your missing man."

"But how did Fraco and him vanish into thin air? We looked and looked and there wasn't a trace."

Stack broke his silence. "Fraco lives in these mountains. He knows them inside and out. Every animal trail, every ravine, every shortcut." He stopped and glanced at Fargo. "Damned peculiar, him missing you twice like he did. Makes me think he was not trying to hit you."

"Cat and mouse," Fargo said.

"That would be my guess," Stack replied. "Fraco has a mean streak bone deep. He is the kind to gut a puppy to watch it die slow."

"Hell," Krupp said.

Stack had more. "It could be he wants us to know he is out there. He wants it to prey on our nerves."

"It will not prey on mine," Cranmeyer declared. "I am getting these wagons through come hell or high water." He reined around. "Come, Mr. Krupp. We will inform the others."

Fargo squinted up at the sun and tiredly rubbed his chin. It had been a long day and it wasn't half over.

"There is something you should know," Stack said.

"Not if it is more bad news."

Stack told him anyway. "About a year ago eleven members of a wagon train were picked off one by one. They never saw who did it. Only one man lived, and he was half dead when he was found. But everyone suspects Fraco was to blame."

"You are saying he might try the same with us."

"We are too big a train for him to wipe us out single-handed. But he might whittle us down some."

Fargo shifted to regard the long line of wagons, drivers

and guards. Which one of them, he wondered, would be next?

"Do you regret coming along?" Stack asked him.

"No." Fargo was glad he played poker a lot.

"Oh? I would have guessed different. Or do you like having your ears buzzed by lead?" Stack pushed his hat back on his head. "It has been hell, and the worst is yet to come."

Skye Fargo agreed.

16

Much to Fargo's surprise, the next two days passed without incident. The freight train wound like so many overfed sheep steadily deeper into the foreboding jaws of the Mimbres Mountains. The crack of bullwhips, the mule skinners constantly bellowing 'Get along, there!', the creak and rattle of the heavily laden wagons, filled the dusty air from dusk until dawn.

Stack shared his surprise. At one point he commented, "If Grind aims to stop us, he will have to do it soon."

What mystified Fargo more was the absence of Fraco. He should be glad the breed did not continue to plague them but he had a feeling in his gut that Fraco had gone off for a reason, and that whatever the reason was, it did not bode well.

Then they came to a virgin valley thick with timber. Cranmeyer called a halt early beside a ribbon of a stream. The wagons were circled, men and animals drank greedily, and the cook caused many a stomach to growl with tantalizing aromas of the stew he was preparing.

Sentries were posted. Everyone was in good if guarded spirits, and there was a lot of smiling and laughing.

Fargo did not join in the festive spirit. He made a circuit of the valley, seeking sign of their enemies. He found nothing to cause alarm. Not so much as a trace of Jefferson Grind or any sign whatsoever of the Mimbres Apaches.

That was another puzzlement.

By now the Mimbres had to be aware the freight train was passing through their territory. Ordinarily, they would send warriors to spy on the train, gauging its strength of arms and whether it was worth the risk of an attack.

Fargo completed his circuit and returned to camp. He should be relieved that he found nothing, but he wasn't. He let the Ovaro drink, then stripped off his saddle and saddle blanket. He was using a rock to pound a picket pin into the ground when shadows fell across him.

"Don't you ever relax?"

Cleopatra, Mavis and Myrtle all wore mischievous grins. Myrtle had removed her sling. She'd mentioned to Fargo that morning that her shoulder was still sore and stiff but she was getting by fairly well.

"I don't ever relax in Apache country," Fargo said.

"They have not hit us yet," Cleopatra said. "If you ask me, they are not going to."

"We have too many guns," Mavis said. "Too many men."

"And women," Myrtle chimed in, and chuckled.

"None of that would not stop the Mimbres," Fargo told them.

Cleopatra swore in mild exasperation. "I swear. You are a wet blanket. Here we are, everything is going well, and you see nothing but storm clouds on our horizon."

"Blue skies don't last forever," Fargo said.

Cleopatra laughed. "Will you listen to yourself? You are doom and gloom up to here." She raised a hand to her chin.

Mavis slid a hand under her shirt and produced a silver flask. "How about if we help you forget your cares and woes?"

Fargo surveyed the camp. He had taken all the precautions it was prudent to take. There was nothing more he could do except wait for the other shoe to drop. Plopping down, he patted his blankets. "Be my guest, ladies."

The sisters grinned and sat facing him. Mavis took a swig and passed the flask.

When it came Fargo's turn, he swallowed with relish. He would dearly love to have a whole bottle. Hell, he would love to be in a saloon somewhere, with a warm dove in his lap and four aces in his hand. Smiling, he held the flask out to them.

"Will you look at this!" Cleopatra said in mock astonishment. "He is human, after all."

"Go to hell," Fargo said.

They all laughed, and Cleo, whose eyes had not left him since they came over, remarked, "This is a pretty little valley. When the moon comes out, it would be nice to go for a walk."

"There might be Mimbres about," Fargo mentioned.

"There might," Cleo agreed, but with a sarcastic edge. "There might be Grind. There might be a bear. There might be a mountain lion. There might be rattlesnakes and spiders and rabid coyotes. But I do not give a good damn. I am not scared of any of them and you should not be either."

"I am only saying," Fargo said.

Cleopatra clucked in disapproval. "I had no idea you were such a worrier. How you have lived so long is beyond me."

But not beyond Fargo. He had lasted as long as he had in a land overrun with cutthroats, hostiles and man-eating beasts because he *was* cautious by nature. "I like breathing," he said.

"I like to pant when the mood suits me," Cleopatra replied, and chortled.

Fargo did not need to be beaten over the head to take her hints. "How about if we go for that walk after supper?"

"That would suit me just fine, tall and handsome. I have an itch that needs scratching."

Mavis looked up. "I lost the coin toss so I will be last."

"You don't have to if you don't want to," Fargo said. She had not sounded very enthused.

"Are you joshing me?" was her rejoinder. "And listen to these two brag about you for the rest of my born days? No, thank you. I aim to find out if you are as terrific as Myrtle claims."

"You three do this a lot," Fargo said. It was a statement, not a question.

"So?" Mavis said. "Oh, I know it's not considered proper. Churchgoing gals look at us as if we are demons. But we make no bones about liking men, or bedding them."

"We do what comes natural," Myrtle remarked. "A body has urges, and we don't deny ours like some women do."

Cleopatra lost some of her good humor. "It gets my goat how some folks brand us as sinners for using our bodies as they are made to be used. If the Almighty didn't want men and women to cuddle, He wouldn't have made us cuddlesome."

Fargo had never looked at it quite like that. "You might have a point," he conceded.

Just then Cranmeyer approached. Krupp, as usual, was in tow. "I want a word with you," he said to Fargo, and gave the Frazier sisters a pointed glance. "Alone, if you ladies don't mind."

"That is twice in the past ten minutes we have been called 'ladies,'" Cleopatra said. "We are no such thing."

"We are women," Myrtle declared.

Cranmeyer appeared puzzled. "There is a difference?"

"There sure as hell is," Mavis said while rising. "Ladies don't spread their legs unless a man licks their feet first. Women do it for the fun."

"The things that come out of your mouths," Cranmeyer said.

"Be careful," Cleopatra warned. "Just because we are not prissy does not give you call to treat us with disrespect."

"When have I ever?" Cranmeyer said. "I am only pointing out that you do not talk like any women I have ever met or am ever likely to meet."

"We will take that as a compliment," Cleopatra said, and impishly pinched his cheek. "Don't keep Fargo long,

122

you hear? Him and me have some special business to attend to later."

The three females ambled toward the nearest campfire.

"Remarkable," Cranmeyer said. Then he gave a toss of his head and sat on the blanket. "But enough about them. We have a weightier matter to discuss. Namely, reaching Silver Lode alive."

Krupp said, "We have made it this far, sir."

Cranmeyer paid him no mind and stared fixedly at Fargo. "I suspect that the attack will come soon. Jefferson Grind has been biding his time. Why he has waited so long to strike is a mystery, but strike he will."

Again Krupp broke in, saying, "Maybe not. Maybe he sees we have too many guns and he doesn't want to tangle with us."

"Do you know the country between here and Silver Lode?" Cranmeyer asked Fargo.

"I have been through it before," Fargo mentioned. As best he could recollect, they had a few more valleys and ridges to cross before they came to a rugged stretch of steep grades and switchbacks.

"If you were Jefferson Grind, where would you jump us?" Cranmeyer wanted to know.

"About ten miles out from Silver Lode," Fargo answered. "Close enough that your drivers and guards think they are almost there and let down their guard, and far enough that the shots and screams won't be heard by anyone *in* Silver Lode."

"I was thinking the same thing," Cranmeyer said. "But then it occurred to me. Grind is sly. He might jump us sooner, thinking we won't expect it."

"There is that," Fargo agreed.

"Which is why I want you to ride out at first light and range on ahead. Sniff out the attack before Grind springs it."

"I will try," was the best Fargo could promise.

"Take Mr. Stack along. Should you run into trouble, he will prove useful."

Fargo would be less conspicuous alone, and said so.

"Perhaps," Cranmeyer said. "But four eyes are better than two, and by your own admission Fraco nearly added you to his long list of victims."

Logic like that was hard to argue with but Fargo did anyway. "You will need him more if we are wrong and the train is struck before we expect."

"A possibility, I grant you," Cranmeyer allowed. "But my mind is made up."

Fargo did not like being told what to do. Even as a boy he had balked at being told to do this or that. When he scouted for the army, as he did on occasion, he always made it plain that he would do his job as he saw fit and not be pushed, prodded or otherwise treated like a fresh recruit.

Cranmeyer was studying him. "I gather you do not approve?"

"I am not taking him, and that is that."

For a few moments Cranmeyer looked disposed to argue. Instead, he wheeled, saying, "Come along, Mr. Krupp."

No sooner did they walk off than a lone figure came toward him wearing a grin fit for a saloon dove. "I was worried they would talk your ear off and spoil our fun." Cleopatra made sure no one was watching and slid the flask partway out of her sleeve. "We can finish this off."

"Your sisters won't mind?"

Cleo tittered. "Hell, they can mind all they want. Fat lot of good it will do them when the bug juice is all gone."

"What happened to share and share alike?" Fargo asked.

"We still do." Cleopatra lowered her voice, and giggled. "But I am not a fanatic about it."

Fargo wondered exactly how much whiskey she had already helped herself to. She passed him the flask. Careful that Cranmeyer and Krupp did not catch him, he took a sip.

"These last few days sure have been boring," Cleopatra commented.

"When you are in Apache country, boring is good."

"I counted on you paying me a visit these past few nights and you didn't show." Cleo did not hide her disappointment.

Fargo admired her full strawberry lips and the delightful curves her clothes could not entirely conceal. "Tonight you get your wish."

"I better," Cleopatra said. "I need a man so bad, I could scream."

"Don't let Cranmeyer hear you say that."

Cleopatra snorted. "Do you think I am loco? He tolerates my sisters and me because we are the best damn mule skinners in the territory. But he does not much like how frank we are about our needs. He is one of those who thinks a woman should be seen and not heard."

Fargo detected a note of hostility. Her next comment confirmed it.

"Men like Cranmeyer annoy the hell out of me. They are cold fish when it comes to sharing their bodies, and have the gall to think everyone should be the same."

"Not everyone likes it as much as we do."

"I am glad you included yourself. But that is as it should be. No two people are alike." Cleo snorted. "Try telling that to the Cranmeyers of the world, though. They think everyone should be exactly like them." She placed her hand on her bullwhip, which was coiled on her right hip. "I would as soon chuck them off a cliff."

"If it bothers you so much, let's not talk about it," Fargo suggested. It would not do to spoil her frame of mind.

Cleo saw right through him. "Don't fret," she smirked. "You will still have a night to remember."

Fargo imagined sliding his hands up under her shirt and felt himself stir below his belt.

Out of the blue Cleo said, "I could never live back in the States. The things they make women do would have me pulling my hair out."

Despite himself, Fargo said, "What things?"

"Always having to wear a dress, for one thing. Always

needing to be prim and proper, for another. Never give men any sass. Spend all day cooking and sewing." Cleopatra actually shuddered. "I would rather be dead than have to do all of that."

Fargo shared her sentiments to a degree. The life of a store clerk or a bank teller was not for him. Doing the same thing day in and day out would torment him worse than having an arrow in his gut.

Simultaneous with his thought, an arrow whizzed out of the night and thudded into the earth a few feet from them.

"What the hell?" Cleopatra blurted. She glanced up, and recoiled. "Oh, my God!

Fargo followed her gaze and his breath caught in his throat.

The arrow had friends.

Barbed shafts were arcing down out of the dark vault of sky, scores of them in a deadly deluge.

17

It was so unexpected that for a fraction of a second Fargo was rooted in shock. Then his instincts took over and he hurled himself at Cleopatra while bawling at the top of his lungs, "Arrows! Take cover!" That was all he got out before the hardwood rain fell.

Cleo bleated in surprise and not a little pain as Fargo slammed into her and bore her to the ground, covering her body with his. He heard the *chuk* of an arrow striking the ground, and then the *chuk-chuk-chuk* blended into so many, there was a continuous loud *CHUK*.

A man screamed. Others cursed. Boots pounded and bedlam broke out, but it lasted only as long as the arrows fell.

In the unnatural silence that followed, Fargo raised his head from Cleopatra's shoulder. She was looking at him strangely, her face twisted in the oddest expression.

An arrow jutted from the soil not an arm's length from their heads. But most of the shafts had fallen farther away, near the two campfires. Incredibly, only one man had been hit and was pinned flat by an arrow through his leg. Everyone else was shaken but all right. Many had sought cover under or in wagons.

"You can get off me now," Cleopatra said in a small voice.

Fargo rolled off and up, palming his Colt. He scanned the sky for more arrows but none appeared.

Others were anxiously doing the same or staring into the surrounding woodland.

Krupp took immediate charge, issuing orders. "Stay close to the wagons! Keep your rifles handy and watch for our attackers! Have that arrow taken out of Baxter and get him under a wagon where he will be safe."

Cranmeyer was looking across the clearing. "Mr. Fargo, will you and Miss Frazier get over here, please?"

Fargo did not like leaving the Ovaro in the open. That was when he noticed that none of the arrows had fallen anywhere near the mules or horses. The animals had been deliberately spared.

"Do you think it was Apaches?" Cranmeyer asked.

"Who else?" But Fargo snatched up one of the arrows and examined it. The way it was made, the feathers, the type of tip, all pointed to one conclusion. "These are Mimbres arrows," he confirmed.

"I never heard of them doing anything like this," Cranmeyer said.

Neither had Fargo. Usually Apaches did not forewarn their quarry with an attack like this.

"It is a miracle none of our stock was hit," Cranmeyer mentioned.

Fargo had been thinking about that. The only reason to spare them was so they could be used to move the wagons. But what possible use would Apaches have for freight wagons? Normally they burned wagons and took their plunder with them.

Cranmeyer turned to the men peering anxiously into the dark. "Anything?" he called out. "Anyone?"

"Not a sign of them!" a driver responded.

"Nothing over here!" yelled a man from across camp.

"This makes no sense," Cranmeyer said. "You would think the Apaches would follow up with an assault."

It made no sense to Fargo, either.

Cleopatra was rubbing her shoulder. "I didn't think Apaches attack much at night."

"They don't," Fargo said. Yet another unusual aspect to this affair.

Cranmeyer tilted his head back. "Why don't they fire more arrows?"

"You *want* them to?" Cleo said.

"Of course not."

Neither did Fargo, but it *was* peculiar that only one barrage of shafts had been unleashed. Almost as if the Apaches had done it to let them know the Apaches were out there. But that was preposterous.

"I am confused," Cleopatra said.

Fargo grunted. She was not alone. But one thing was clear. "From here on out we can't afford any mistakes. Now that the Mimbres have found us, they will do their damnedest to stop us from reaching Silver Lode."

"They are welcome to try," Cranmeyer heatedly declared. He grew thoughtful. "But maybe there is a silver lining to this storm cloud."

"A silver lining to Apaches?" Cleopatra said, and laughed.

"There is if the Mimbres should come across Jefferson Grind and his men. The Mimbres will wipe them out, giving us one less worry."

"I wouldn't count on that, Tim," Cleo told him.

"You are a bundle of optimism," Cranmeyer said sourly, and turned away. "Excuse me. I must see to securing the camp."

Cleo put her hands on her hips. "How he can be so calm is beyond me." She gazed sadly at Fargo. "Damn those Apaches, anyhow. They have gone and spoiled our fun."

Fargo nodded. They were not about to slip from camp to indulge their hunger for each other now. It would have to wait.

Her sisters were approaching. Cleopatra went to meet them, saying, "Talk to you later, handsome."

"Later," Fargo echoed, and hurried to the Ovaro. Although no more arrows had rained down he was not about to take it for granted they wouldn't. He threw on his saddle blanket and saddle, tightened the cinch, tied on his bedroll and saddlebags and led the Ovaro over next to a wagon where the high canvas would shield it from shafts.

The center of the camp was deserted save for the cook and a few others. The cook was putting a fresh pot of coffee on to boil.

Men were under every freight wagon, each with a rifle and a brace of pistols. Cranmeyer was going from one to the next, offering encouragement.

All they could do was wait.

Then Stack materialized out of the shadows. "Are you in the mood for a little excitement?"

"I have had enough for one night," Fargo said.

Stack nodded at the night-mantled terrain. "I was thinking that you and me could scout around. Find out exactly how many Apaches we are up against, and what they are up to."

"They are waiting for daybreak to attack," was Fargo's guess.

"We need to be sure."

"I am fine right here," Fargo said. He knew what Stack was leading up to, and he did not want any part of it.

"Look. You and me are the only two here with much experience at this. It has to be us."

Fargo swore under his breath.

"All we have to do is find out who is leading this band and kill him and the rest will scatter."

"Is that all?"

Stack squatted and commenced removing his spurs. "Do you want to separate or stick together?"

"Stick," Fargo said. "Leave your rifle here. We will use our knives unless we are spotted."

Grinning, Stack drew his knife from his hip sheath and tested the edge by lightly running it across a finger. A thin line of blood welled up. "I am ready and raring to go."

"What the hell are you so happy about?" Fargo demanded. "These are Apaches, not Shoshones." The Shoshones were a friendly tribe, *the* friendliest, by most accounts.

Cranmeyer took the news of what they were about to do with a nod of approval. "It would be nice to know what we are up against. But you two be careful out there."

"Pass the word to your men," Fargo said. He did not want to be shot by their own people.

"This is a brave thing you are doing."

"It is what you pay us for," Stack said.

Fargo did not say anything.

The night was as still as a cemetery. The valley, awash in star glow, was a pale snake twisting along the base of steep slopes.

Fargo and Stack crawled under a wagon and rose into crouches on the other side. Stack grinned and wagged his knife as if eager to use it. Fargo frowned, and wondered.

The trick was to reach the vegetation without the Apaches spotting them. It helped that there was no moon. Otherwise, they might as well carry signs that read, HERE WE ARE! KILL US!

Fargo went first. Flattening, he crawled toward a waist-high boulder. At least, he *thought* it was, but when he got there he discovered it was a clump of bushes in shadow. He started to rise to his knees and thought better of it. *These are Apaches!* he scolded himself.

White men who had never fought them could not fully appreciate what it was like. Apaches were ghosts given human guise, two-legged predators who pounced at the first hint of weakness. As quick as mountain lions, as slippery as snakes, and as wise as bears, they were the masters of their domain.

No one was immune from their depredations. When those depredations started was anyone's guess. The Mexicans complained of Apache raids long before the coming of the white man, and the Spaniards wrote of Apache atrocities long before the Mexicans.

The Apaches did not call themselves "Apaches."

Among themselves they were the "People of the Woods." To everyone else they were killers with a capital K.

Fargo shut all that from his mind. The Arkansas toothpick was in his right hand. He held it so the blade was under his forearm and would not reflect the starlight and give him away. He moved silently, or as near to silent as a man could move. Stack was on his right, and almost as quiet.

The breeze on Fargo's face was so soft and soothing that he could almost forget where he was and what he was doing. Almost. The yip of a coyote that might not be a coyote reminded him.

They crawled twenty feet, and nothing happened. Thirty feet. Clear out to fifty, but they were the only signs of life. Either the Apaches had left or were well back from the wagons. Fargo hoped it was the former. He could do without pitting his sinews against warriors whose bodies were iron from head to toe.

Once again Fargo shut his mind to his mental ramblings. If he wasn't careful, he would think himself into an early grave. Or to being tortured.

The Apaches were adept at it. Not all that long ago they tied several Mexicans upside down to wagon wheels and lit fires under them to bake their brains. A cavalry officer had his eyes and tongue removed and was left to wander the desert in blind, mute despair. It was said Apaches tortured people to test their mettle. It was also said Apaches delighted in the suffering.

Whichever the case, the Apaches were not the only tribe who did it. Some did worse. The Hurons, but one example, perpetrated atrocities that made the Apaches seem tame.

Then there were white men. Their record was far from spotless. They scalped; they tortured; they slew women and children. During the war with the Creeks, none other than Davy Crockett reported that a lodge filled with Creeks was set on fire and the Creeks burned alive.

Later, those with Crockett helped themselves to a store of potatoes found under the charred remains—potatoes smeared with the fat and juices of the burned Creeks.

Again Fargo caught himself. He must focus. He must concentrate. He glanced at Stack and motioned and Stack immediately crawled to the right while Fargo crept to the left. His intent was to circle the camp. If the Apaches were there, Stack or he would find them.

It did not seem possible the Apaches had left. Why launch a flight of arrows, then retreat without cause? Unless there was more to it. Maybe the Apaches *did* want them to know they were there, as incredible as that seemed. Maybe the arrows were to keep them on edge so they did not get much sleep.

Apaches were clever that way.

Something on the ground caught Fargo's eye. He inched toward it, his arm poised to thrust.

It was an arrow. Two of the feathers were missing. Apparently an Apache had left it there. But that, too, was peculiar. Arrows took hours to make. The right wood had to be found, then trimmed and smoothed so the shaft was round and straight. The point and the feathers had to be attached. Warriors did not just throw them away. Especially when the missing feathers on the one Fargo found could easily be replaced.

Perplexed, he crawled on. At a slight noise he held his breath and strained his ears but the sound was not repeated.

The things he got himself into, Fargo reflected. He did not want to be there. He had not wanted to have anything to do with the freight train. But then he met the Frazier sisters, all three beyond compare, all three as playful as women could be and not be working in a fancy house in Denver.

Fargo almost sighed. Once again his lust had gotten the better of him. But he could no more refuse a pretty female than he could flap his arms and fly.

Another sound caused him to stop cold and imitate a

log. Something, or someone, was coming toward him, slinking over the ground like an oversized lizard. He tensed, then saw who it was. "You."

"Me," Stack said. His face was caked with sweat. "Any sign of them? Anything at all?"

"They are gone."

Stack swore, then whispered, "What in hell is going on? If you know, tell me."

"If I knew, I would."

"What now?"

"We wait until morning." Fargo wished dawn had already broken. Fear was easier to keep in check in the day than in the dark.

"All I know is I am sick and tired of waiting for something to happen. I will be glad when the killing begins."

The hell of it was, Fargo thought to himself, that might be awful damn soon.

18

Everyone was up a half hour before daybreak, as usual. Coffee was put on, as usual, and while the cook prepared eggs and bacon, the mule teams were hitched to the wagons, as usual. Then everyone sat down to eat, as usual, and shortly after sunrise the freight train was on the move, as usual.

But there was nothing usual about the way the drivers and the guards were acting. Normally, they would talk and be friendly to one another. But this morning they were surly and sour and no one cracked so much as a smile. The Frazier sisters kept to themselves, snapping at anyone who came near them.

"No one got hardly a lick of sleep," Krupp commented to Fargo, Cranmeyer and Stack. "They are in no shape for a fight."

"We have the Apaches to thank," Timothy P. Cranmeyer said. "And those infernal arrows of theirs."

"Everyone is tired," Stack stated the obvious.

Fargo's mouth became a slit. "Tired makes for careless." Which could be exactly what the Apaches wanted.

"I will advise them to be on their guard," Cranmeyer said, and walked off to do just that, Krupp at his elbow.

"Why do I feel as if I am standing under a cliff and it is about to come crashing down on me?" Stack asked. He was not addressing Fargo. He was asking himself.

Fargo had the same feeling. He stepped into the stirrups and lifted the reins. Drivers were climbing on wagons and guards were checking weapons. Bullwhips cracked, and the lead wagons lumbered into motion.

Tapping his spurs, Fargo rode on ahead. The weight of his responsibility bore down heavily on his shoulders. He was on point. It was up to him to spot an ambush before the ambush was sprung. The consequences, if he slipped up, were too dire to contemplate.

Fargo's mouth was dry, and he had barely started out. The temperature had yet to begin its climb toward uncomfortable.

Birds chirped and warbled, and a solitary doe went bounding off in fright.

Fargo reviewed the precautions he had taken. He had told Stack to make sure the outriders stayed close to the wagons. No drifting, and no talking. Those at the rear were not to fall behind. The wagon guards were to have cartridges in the chambers of their rifles. The drivers were not to stop for any reason short of Armageddon.

Now it was up to fate. Unfortunately, fate was a notoriously fickle mistress. A cruel mistress, on occasion.

Fargo scanned the road and the valley and the ridge beyond and saw no cause for alarm. But that was the thing with Apaches. There was never cause for alarm until it was too late and the alarm would do no good.

A bend hid Fargo from the train. He put his hand on his Colt. He had a hunch that whatever the Apaches were up to would come later in the day. The longer the Apaches waited, the more the strain on the drivers and guards, and the more likely they were taken unawares.

Based on the number of arrows let loose on them the night before, Fargo figured there must be upward of forty Apaches. That was an awful lot of Apaches. More than enough, if they planned it well, to decimate the train before the guards got off a shot.

The sun climbed and the heat climbed with it.

A rattlesnake crossed the road in front of them. Overhead, a hawk was hunting.

Sweat trickled down Fargo's back, and got into eyes.

A swipe of his sleeve spared his eyes from stinging, but only for a bit.

Suddenly hooves drummed behind him, and Fargo shifted in the saddle to find Stack hurrying to catch up. "What are you doing here?" he demanded the instant the hired killer drew rein. "You were supposed to stay with the wagons."

"Cranmeyer sent me," Stack said. "He said to tell you that he is in charge and he will do as he damn well pleases."

Fargo scowled. "How are the others holding up?"

"Most can barely stay awake," Stack said. "At noon we should let them catch quick naps if they want." He paused. "Do you want me to go back or can I ride with you?"

"You have come this far," Fargo said, and hoped to hell he was wrong about what he was thinking.

The road narrowed as they wound up out of the valley. At the top of the ridge it widened again. On either side was open space sprinkled with bushes. They drew rein and looked back.

"This is a good spot for the wagons to stop," Stack said.

"It is too soon," Fargo said. Noon was hours off yet. "We will keep going."

"It is a good spot for a lot of things," Stack went on. He spoke so casually and drew so casually that Fargo did not realize he was holding the Remington until it was pointed at him. "Go another fifty feet or so and stop."

"What is the idea?"

Stack's smile was empty of warmth. "You are not dumb and I am not dumb, so let's not act like we are."

"Can I ask why?"

"Is there any why but money? A whole hell of a lot of it. Jefferson Grind has deep pockets. He pays a lot better than Cranmeyer." Stack wagged the Colt. "Get moving."

Fargo complied. "You have been his man from the beginning?"

"I was his before Cranmeyer hired me," Stack revealed. "Grind wanted someone with the freight train. He picked me."

Fargo went as far as he had been told, and stopped. "What now? A bullet to my brain and you wait for the train?"

"It is the smart thing to do," Stack said. "But if Cranmeyer does not see you with me when he comes over that ridge, he might become suspicious. And we do not want that."

Fargo surveyed the road and the open space on either side. An awful premonition came over him. "We?"

"I have friends in low places," Stack said, and grinned.

"The drivers and guards have families, some of them. Wives and children." Fargo sought to dissuade him.

"What in hell do I care? With me it is the money and only the money."

"You had me fooled," Fargo admitted. "A little."

"I could tell it was not a hundred percent," Stack said. "So I made it a point to make you think your instincts were wrong and it worked."

"Jefferson Grind will be proud."

"Him?" Stack snorted. "He doesn't give a damn so long as the job gets done. He wants this over with so he can claim the crown of freight king of the whole territory, or some such silliness."

"He will make enough money to start his own bank," Fargo said. Grind would have a monopoly and could charge as much as he dared to get away with.

"That will still not be enough. He hankers after wealth and power like you do after women."

Fargo stared at the Remington. It was as steady as a rock.

"Don't force me," Stack said.

Fargo had noticed that the nearest cover was fifty yards distant. "You picked a poor spot for an ambush."

"I didn't pick it. Fraco did. And it is a perfect spot if you know anything about Apaches."

"Apaches?" Fargo repeated, and something about the sly look that came over Stack caused invisible fingers to twist his guts. "The Mimbres and Grind? Working together?"

"Afraid so," Stack replied. "It is the ace Grind had up his sleeve. The one you said Wilson mentioned. Damn him to hell."

Fargo broke out in a sweat that was not due to the heat. "Apaches would never work with a white man."

"They do when they are friends with a half-breed who has lived among them, and the white man hires that same half-breed to go to the Apaches and promise them plenty of other whites to kill and all the plunder they could want."

"Fraco," Fargo said.

"He is the key to all of this. Thanks to him, Grind will not be blamed. The Apaches will."

"It has been well thought out," Fargo stalled while prodding his brain for a way to turn the tables.

"Grind's doing. He is a thinker, that one."

Fargo wished he was. He almost lunged to try and knock Stack from the saddle so he could race to the train and warn them. He would have, too, if not for that rock-steady Remington.

Stack caught him staring at it. "That reminds me. Hand over your Colt. Two fingers only. And if you know what is good for you, you will pretend you are molasses."

"Not the gun belt?" Fargo stalled some more.

Shaking his head, Stack said, "Cranmeyer might notice you are not wearing it, and I don't want him suspicious." He chuckled. "Not that it would do him any good. We have enough Apaches to wipe him out twice over."

"They are well hid." Fargo figured the warriors were off amid the trees and boulders.

"You don't know the half of it," Stack said. "But you will soon enough."

"Where is Grind? I would like to meet him."

"Forget him. You should be thinking about this."

Stack wagged the Remington. "And what I am going to do to you with it if you don't hand over that six-shooter like I told you to."

With the utmost reluctance, Fargo used two fingers to pluck the Colt by the grips and slowly ease it from his holster. He just as slowly held it out. They were too far apart for Stack to reach it so he kneed the Ovaro, saying, "Here. Take it."

The Remington didn't waver. "To tell you the truth, I did not think you would be so easy."

By then they were close enough, and Fargo had slipped his right boot from the stirrup. "I am happy to disappoint you," he said. He swung his leg up and out. His toe caught Stack's wrist and knocked the Remington aside, and in the blink of an eye he launched himself from the saddle. His shoulder slammed into Stack and they tumbled.

He lost his hold on the Colt.

Stack was swearing.

Fargo hit on his side and pushed up onto his knees a split second before Stack did. Stack was trying to level the Remington and Fargo discouraged him with a hard chop to the jaw that snapped Stack's head back. He cocked his fist to do it again but a boot heel caught him in the stomach and knocked him onto his back.

Fargo had expected Stack to be tough. The man was whipcord and iron. The same heel stomped at his face and he rolled out of the way. Stack kicked at him again. This time Fargo dodged and swung his legs in a quick loop that caught Stack across the chest.

Fargo saw his Colt. He dived, his palm molding to the grips. Twisting, he thumbed back the hammer. The shock in Stack's eyes was priceless; no one had ever beaten him before.

"I will give your regards to Jefferson Grind," Fargo made the mistake of gloating. Without warning, strong hands seized his arms and he was slammed flat. A knee was rammed into his chest, pinning him, even as his legs were pinned.

A quartet of swarthy faces loomed above his.

Cold steel glittered and was raised on high.

"No killing!" Stack said. "We need him alive."

The warrior with the knife checked his stab. He wore a breechclout and a faded gray shirt. A wide headband and knee-high moccasins completed his wardrobe. His features might have been chiseled from granite for all the emotion he showed. "You do not want him dead?"

"Didn't you hear me?" Stack said. "We need him alive to trick the other whites."

Fargo stopped struggling.

Three of the warriors holding him were Mimbres Apaches. The fourth man, the man with the knife, was a mix of red and white; the dark brown eyes of an Apache but the light sandy hair of a white man; the high cheekbones and hairless chin of an Apache but skin that was not quite as dark as that of his three companions.

"Fraco," Fargo said.

Hearing his name, the breed glanced down. "You are the one Cuchillo Negro talks about. The white who rides many trails."

Alarm spiked Fargo. "Cuchillo Negro is with you?"

"He did not come," Fraco said. "He thinks the white-eye called Grind use the Shis-Inday."

That sounded like Cuchillo Negro to Fargo. "You *are* being used," Fargo grasped at a straw. "Grind is using you to kill his enemy and have you take the blame."

"Not me," Fraco said, and smiled an oily smile. "Them," he said, nodding at the three warriors and then gesturing to the right and left of the road.

"Do the Mimbres know they will be blamed for this?" Fargo probed. He very much doubted it.

Fraco grinned. "I told them the white-eye called Cranmeyer is their enemy and they must stop his wagons or a great many more whites will come to their mountains and take over their land."

"You can't stop Cranmeyer with the handful you have here," Fargo tried another tack.

Fraco's grin widened.

The three Mimbres hauled Fargo to his feet. He was not quite up when they shoved him toward the Ovaro and he nearly stumbled. Biting off his fury, he gripped the saddle horn to pull himself up.

Stack was covering him with the Remington. "One wrong move," he said.

Fargo debated the odds of swinging up and galloping off without taking a slug. They were not good. The saddle creaked under him as he swung up and glared at Stack. "There. Are you hap—" He stopped, frozen in surprise.

Fraco and the three Mimbres were gone.

19

It was said Apaches were not quite human. It was said they were savage and merciless. The only good Apache was a dead Apache was another common saying, but the whites who said that usually applied it to all Indians.

It was said Apaches were ghosts. That they could appear and disappear at will. That when they struck, they struck out of nowhere, and then vanished before anyone could lay a hand on them.

The truth of the matter was that Apaches really *could* appear and disappear at will. When they struck, they *did* strike out of nowhere. And they invariably vanished before anyone could lay a hand on them.

But they were not ghosts. They were human. They were warriors as tough as the land they roamed. They were men as hard as men could be, and if they seemed ghostlike, it was due to abilities they honed from an early age. Remarkable abilities, such as being able to cover seventy miles on foot without tiring. Or to move in complete silence. Or to kill in the blink of an eye.

Another of their abilities had to do with their vanishing into thin air, as it so often seemed.

Fargo had seen it demonstrated once by an Apache scout at a fort. The colonel in charge thought it wise for his new troops to know what they were up against so he had asked the scout to show them.

Simply put, an Apache could hide himself in virtually any terrain in a span of seconds. A small bush, a small boulder, a log, objects that did not look big enough to hide a kitten, could hide an Apache. If no cover was handy, they would scoop shallow holes into which they swiftly curled and then covered themselves with the dirt they had scooped. To the casual eye, the ground appeared to be as it should be. But when a hapless white happened by, up sprang the Apache.

So when Fraco and the three Apaches disappeared, Fargo knew the terrible truth. Dread seized him. He studied the open ground on both sides of the rutted road and noticed little things he had not paid much attention to before. Swirls in the dirt where there should not be swirls. Bumps where there should not be bumps. Bushes that were darker than they should be because the sun passing through them was blocked by something on the other side.

"Hell."

Stack laughed at that. "Just caught on, didn't you? And you are supposed to be so sharp."

Fargo simmered but said nothing.

"There will be a lot of dead here shortly," Stack said smugly. He shifted in the saddle toward the trees to the south, and waved.

A rider appeared. On either side of him were others, grim men with guns. A heavyset man in the middle returned the gesture.

The riders were all white.

The heavyset man wore a wide-brimmed straw hat and city clothes more fit for the opera than range riding. A gold ring on his finger flashed in the sunlight. A watch chain adorned his vest.

"Who?" Fargo asked as they melted back into the vegetation.

"That would be the great Jefferson Grind himself," Stack said. "At least he is great in his own mind if no one else's."

"You don't seem to think highly of the gent who hired you," Fargo brought up.

"There is no 'seem' to it," Stack said. "He is a pig.

144

But he is a pig who is paying me a lot of money so I will keep the pig comments to myself."

"If you work for a pig, what does that make you?"

Stack colored and leaned on his saddle horn. "I do what he pays me to do and that is it."

Fargo was curious. "The other day when you offered to help me hunt down Fraco, you came along to make sure I didn't catch him."

Stack nodded.

"And last night when we were crawling around, you helped to make sure all the Apaches had gone off as they were supposed to?"

"You are slow but you catch on."

"And those four men, Wilson and Becker and the others—?"

"They were on their way to meet with me." Stack gazed to the east and cocked his head, listening. "I wanted to put a bullet or two into Cranmeyer but Grind insists on doing that himself."

"You were slick," Fargo admitted.

"I am paid to be."

"There was something about you that didn't sit right," Fargo said. "Something at the back of my mind that warned me I couldn't trust you. But I didn't listen."

"We should always trust our instincts," Stack said. "They keep our hair on our heads and our breath in our lungs." He cocked his head again. "Do you hear that?"

Fargo had been hearing it for some time; the creak and rattle of heavy wagons, the clomp of hooves and voices. The wagon train was climbing the last grade to the top of the ridge. It would not be long before the first of the wagons rumbled into view.

Fargo thought fast. He had mere minutes in which to thwart Jefferson Grind. But what could he hope to do when he was one against so many? How could he warn Cranmeyer without sacrificing his own life?

Stack was enormously pleased with himself. "I will make more money from this one job than I made all last year."

"Good for you."

"After this is over I think I will drift down Mexico way," Stack said. "Find me a cantina somewhere, with a pretty senorita, and spend a month or two drinking tequila. How does that sound?"

Fargo had an inspiration. It was not much, as inspirations went, but it was all he could think of. "You are scum," he said.

"Now, now," Stack scolded, as if Fargo were ten. "There is no call for talk like that."

"You are scum through and through." Fargo expanded on his insult. "At least the Apaches have an excuse for the killing they do. You don't have any. You are a weasel with a fancy revolver, nothing more."

"I am warning you," Stack said, glaring. "You do not want to make me mad."

"We are known by the company we keep, and you keep the company of a pig like Jefferson Grind and a bastard like Fraco."

Stack raised the Remington. "Damn you."

"Go ahead. Pull the trigger on that smoke wagon," Fargo taunted. "I am unarmed. It should be easy for a coward."

"I'm not yellow!" Stack practically shouted. Too late, he realized what he had done, and stiffened. With an oath he glanced toward where the road came over the ridge.

The point riders and the first wagon had appeared.

Cranmeyer and Krupp were out in front with several guards, and had drawn rein in puzzlement.

Stack jerked his revolver down, and swore. He was so mad, he gnashed his teeth. "You tricky son of a bitch."

Not tricky enough, Fargo thought. He had given Cranmeyer the idea that something was wrong, and the train had stopped. But now what? How could he save the drivers and guards? To say nothing of the Frazier sisters. The answer was obvious; he couldn't. No matter what he did, Grind and the Apaches would attack. The best he could do, the best he could hope for, was to warn them

146

so they had a few precious seconds in which to bring their weapons to bear. Those seconds might make all the difference.

Fargo smiled at Stack. "Is it true your mother was a whore?"

"What?"

"Is it true she slept with half the Fifth Cavalry and you don't know who your father was?"

Stack blinked. "What the hell are you up to?" He did not wait for an answer. "Let me guess. You are trying to provoke me. You want me good and mad so I will shoot you or hit you. But it won't work. I am not ten years old. Cranmeyer will not catch on that something is wrong."

"He already has," Fargo said, and nodded.

Krupp was riding toward them, all six feet plus and two hundred pounds or more of him. His right hand rested on the butt of his Colt, and he kept glancing from Fargo to Stack and back again. Ten feet from them he drew rein. "What is going on here?" he demanded.

"Why didn't Cranmeyer come with you?" Stack asked.

"I told him not to," Krupp said.

"*You* told him?" Stack said. "Since when do you give him orders? He is the boss."

"You forget I am the captain of his freight train. I see to it that no harm comes to him."

"Oh, you do, do you?" Stack sounded amused.

Krupp nodded. "Because I am big, some folks seem to think that must mean I am slow. But I am not slow. I just don't say a lot. I keep my own peace."

Fargo wanted to warn him. But Stack was holding the pearl-handled Remington close to his leg, and all Stack had to do was angle the barrel and squeeze the trigger.

"What are you getting at?" the killer snapped at the captain.

"I give the orders and I ask the questions," Krupp said. "And I will ask you again. What is going on here?"

"This is a good spot to noon," Stack said. "We have been waiting for you, is all."

"Why is your six-shooter out?"

Stack shrugged. "This is Apache country. A man doesn't need any more reason than that, does he?"

"I suppose not." Krupp started to wheel his bay but stopped with the animal broadside to them. His right arm, Fargo noticed, was screened by his body. "What about the other one?"

"Eh?" Stack said.

"Fargo's six-shooter," Krupp said. "His holster is empty. What happened to his revolver?"

Fargo almost told him that an Apache had taken it, but Stack responded first.

"How the hell should I know? You ask a lot of damn fool questions." Stack looked toward the woods that hid Jefferson Grind and his men, then at the seemingly open ground that hid Fraco and the Mimbres Apaches. "Holler to Cranmeyer and tell him to bring the wagons up."

"Did you know I was in the army?" Krupp asked.

It was Stack's day for saying, "What?"

"I was in the army before I came to work for Mr. Cranmeyer. A sergeant in the infantry." Krupp smiled in fond recollection. "I liked military life, liked it a lot."

"I do not care," Stack said.

"You will in a minute," Krupp assured him. "You see, Mr. Cranmeyer needed a captain for his freight trains. He needed someone who can organize things so they run smoothly. Someone used to giving orders. Someone who can handle men and drill them the way the army does."

"And he picked you? How wonderful," Stack said with deliberate scorn. "But what does any of that have to do with anything?"

"I make a good captain because I was a good sergeant," Krupp said. "I was good with the men under me. I learned which ones I could depend on and which ones I couldn't. Which ones I could trust and which ones were liable to turn tail in a fight." He paused. "I have never trusted you. Not from the moment you hired on with us until now."

Stack grew rigid with wariness. "Why bring that up all of a sudden?" he asked suspiciously.

"I want you to understand," Krupp said.

"Understand what?" Stack impatiently snapped.

"I want you to understand that you did not pull the wool over my eyes," Krupp said. "I want you to understand why I killed you." And with that, his right hand rose and in it was his Colt.

Stack was ungodly quick. He leveled the Remington and snapped off a shot first.

Krupp jerked, and fired. He had been hit but he got off a shot and he did not shoot for the chest as Stack had done; he shot Stack in the head. Even as he squeezed the trigger he slapped those big legs of his against his bay and bawled, "Ride, Fargo! Ride!"

Fargo did not need encouragement. A bellow of rage had risen from the trees and the earth was sprouting Apaches as if they were cornstalks. He used his spurs and bent low and was glad he had when an arrow cleaved the air above him. Only then did he realize that Cranmeyer and the men who had been with him were nowhere to been seen. They had gone back down the ridge. The first wagon was still there, parked so it blocked the road, but the driver and the wagon guard were not in it.

Jefferson Grind and his hired killers were charging from the trees, Grind conspicuous by his straw hat, but they were too far off to keep Fargo and Krupp from getting away.

Not so the Apaches. There had to be twenty warriors on either side, dirt and dust cascading from their bronzed bodies as they rose from concealment. Several were close enough to stop them, and bounded to do so. Others let fly with arrows. Rifles belched lead and smoke.

An arrow embedded itself in Krupp's bay but the horse kept going. Krupp blasted a Mimbres who sprang at him with a knife.

Fargo had problems of his own. An arrow sliced his shoulder but did not stick. A bullet nicked his hat. A warrior reared in front of him, taking aim with a Sharps, and he rode the Apache down. At the last instant the Mimbres tried to leap aside but the Ovaro bowled him over as if he were a rag doll. Bone crunched and blood splattered, and then Fargo was in the clear and the Ovaro was nose to tail with the bay.

"Kill them!" Jefferson Grind roared. "Kill them all!"

Fraco shouted something in the Apache tongue.

Yipping in wolfish chorus, the warriors covered the ground in long bounds, swooping to the attack.

20

Surprise had piled on surprise ever since Fargo rode into Hot Springs. And a new one awaited him as he swept over the ridge and started down the slope. He had imagined that Cranmeyer and the drivers and guards were fleeing. It was the sensible thing to do, confronted as they were by the combined force of Jefferson Grind and his men, and the Apache war party.

But Fargo was amazed to see that they hadn't fled. Instead, all the drivers and the guards, the Frazier sisters included, were forming into rows. Six abreast, rifles at their shoulders. Much as the army would do.

Krupp's doing, no doubt. The former sergeant galloped up to them and vaulted down. He stumbled and nearly fell, either from haste or from his wound. He had one hand pressed to a dark stain on his side where Stack had shot him.

Fargo flew on around the ranks and drew rein behind them.

"Remember what I taught you!" Krupp bellowed. "Hold formation! Stand your ground and give them hell!" He whipped his hand overhead. "Front line, on your knees. Volley fire at my command!"

The Apaches and Jefferson Grind's killers swept down the ridge in no formation at all. Each man, red and white, had only one thing in mind, and that was to reach the freighters and wreak mayhem.

"Front line, fire!" Krupp shouted.

Six rifles thundered, spitting flame and lead. Instantly, the six began to replace the spent cartridges.

Only three Apaches pitched to the earth, and one did not move again after he struck.

"Second line, fire!"

Six more rifles boomed. This time the men took better aim, and warriors broke stride or went down.

Neither Jefferson Grind nor any of his men, who were behind the Mimbres, were hit.

"Third line," Krupp roared. "At my order, fire!"

For a third time the freighters banged off shots, and five of the six scored.

Even so, there were plenty of Apaches and all of Grind's killers left. The onrushing wave was set to wash over the defenders when the remarkable occurred—the Apaches stopped and wheeled and sped back up the slope, taking their wounded and dead with them.

"What the hell?" Timothy P. Cranmeyer blurted.

"They are leaving!" a driver cried in astonishment.

Of course they were, Fargo reflected. Apaches were not idiots. They always planned their ambushes with the utmost care so that few if any of their number were slain. None of those warriors wanted to die. And now that they had lost the element of surprise and the tide of battle had turned against them, they were doing what anyone with any intelligence would do.

If the freighters were astounded, Jefferson Grind and his men were positively flabbergasted. They reined up in a body and watched Apaches race by.

"What the hell?" Grind echoed Cranmeyer.

"Where do they think they are going?" one of his men yelled.

The Apaches did not so much as glance at them. They were intent on reaching safety before they took a bullet in the back.

But the freighters did not let loose with another volley. Krupp had shouted for them to hold their fire. Some of the men glanced at him as if he were not in his right mind, but when one of them brought his rifle up, Krupp roared for him to lower it.

Fargo had not thought much of Krupp until now. The quiet, unassuming captain had not seemed equal to the challenge of reaching Silver Lode safely. But he had proven more than capable. Army sergeants had a habit of doing that.

A general cry from the freighters drew Fargo's attention to Jefferson Grind's bunch. They were reluctantly turning tail. Without their Apache allies they were hopelessly outnumbered and in a pitched fight would be wiped out.

Several of Cranmeyer's guards ran toward their horses to give chase but were stopped by a shout from Krupp.

"Stand fast! No one goes anywhere unless I say so!"

"But they are escaping!" a man protested.

"Breaking ranks might be just what the Apaches want us to do," Krupp responded. "They will turn on us and overrun us faster than you can spit."

"But—" another man began.

Cranmeyer broke him off with, "You will do as Mr. Krupp says! The important thing is not killing Apaches! The important thing is to get my freight wagons through!"

Fargo was content to stay put. He had nothing against the Apaches. But then Jefferson Grind glanced over his shoulder, his face a mask of raw hatred, as another rider came up alongside him.

That other rider was Fraco.

Fargo's legs seemed to move of their own accord. His spurs raked the Ovaro and he was off in pursuit. He heard Cranmeyer and one of the Frazier sisters call his name but he didn't stop.

There was something Cranmeyer was overlooking.

Yes, the Apaches were fleeing *now*, but they might reorganize and attack the freight train again later on. Especially if Jefferson Grind, through Fraco, was able to convince them that a second try would succeed.

Fargo could not let that happen. He bent to shuck the Henry from the saddle scabbard and happened to set eyes on a slain Apache. Near the warrior's outstretched fingers was his Colt. Hauling on the reins, he leaped down, scooped the Colt up, and vaulted back into the saddle. He lost only a dozen seconds, but by the time he reached the crest, few of the Apaches were in sight.

Jefferson Grind and his men were galloping to the west along the road.

Shoving the Colt into his holster, Fargo knuckled down to the task of overtaking them. He was surprised they had not noticed him. Since none of the freighters had given immediate chase, Grind must not anticipate pursuit.

That there were eleven of them, plus Grind and Fraco, was not a factor to take lightly, and Fargo didn't. All he wanted was a clear shot. Actually, two clear shots.

They disappeared around a bend.

Fargo pushed the Ovaro, anxious to get within rifle range. He was almost to the bend when caution compelled him to slow the stallion to a walk even though he did not want to. He came to where he could see the next stretch of road, and drew rein.

Grind and his men had stopped.

Fully twenty Apaches barred their way. To judge by the hard voices and angry gestures, an argument was taking place. Fraco appeared to be translating.

Fargo could not quite make out what was being said. He was at a loss until one of the warriors pointed at Grind and made a comment that caused Jefferson Grind to explode.

"It's not my fault, damn you! How was I to know? Our plan should have worked!"

The Apaches were upset. They did not like it that some of their warriors had been killed and wounded, and they held Grind to blame. The ambush had been his idea. He promised them an easy kill and plenty of plunder, and instead they had found themselves rushing into the waiting guns of an enemy who was ready for them. To their way of thinking, Grind had misled them. And

Apaches did not like to be misled. They did not like it at all.

A stout Apache said something to Fraco, who translated too quietly for Fargo to overhear. But he did hear Jefferson Grind's outraged swearing.

"He dares to threaten *me*? After I went and tried to do his people a favor?"

Fraco said something that made Jefferson Grind madder.

"To hell with him! I will not sit here and be insulted. Not by no savage, I won't!"

Once more Fraco spoke in that quiet way of his.

"I don't care!" Jefferson Grind declared. "Tell him anyway! Then have him and the rest of these devils get out of our way."

Fraco seemed to make some sort of appeal to Grind.

"I will not! And need I remind you that you work for me? You will do as I say to do."

The stout Apache got tired of waiting for an answer and angrily growled at Fraco.

It looked to Fargo as if the breed was loath to translate.

Then Fraco shrugged and evidently imparted whatever Grind had instructed him to say.

For a few moments the stout Apache glared at Jefferson Grind. Then he turned away as if the matter were settled. But he was not all the way around when he let out with a sharp cry in the Mimbres tongue, and just like that, violence erupted.

To a warrior, the Apaches threw themselves at the whites. Grind's bunch cut loose with their hardware. Some of the Apaches were hit but the rest reached Grind and his men, seeking to slay or unhorse each rider.

Bedlam ensued.

It was every man for himself. The Apaches fought with the ferocity for which they were widely feared, while the whites fought for their lives.

Rifles and revolvers thundered. Arrows and knives pierced flesh. Blood spurted, sprayed, misted. Horses added to the bedlam by rearing and plunging. Some were brought crashing down, their legs nearly severed. Their whinnies mixed with the shouts and oaths and war cries of the frenziedly battling humans.

Fargo stayed where he was. He wanted no part of it. The truth be told, his sympathies were with the Mimbres, but they would kill him if he showed himself.

A white man screeched as his head was split like a melon. A warrior went down with a hole between his eyes.

Death, death and more death, amid a whirl of confusion and the din of brutal conflict.

Fargo was so engrossed in the battle that he nearly lost his own skin. The crunch of a moccasin on loose pebbles was his only warning. He twisted just as a lone warrior launched himself at him. Fargo started to bring up the Henry but he was catapulted free of the stirrups by a battering ram. Or that was how it felt when the Apache's shoulder caught him in the belly. A knife slashed at his throat. That it missed was not through any effort on his part.

Fargo crashed onto his side and the Henry went skittering. He had the presence of mind to roll and came up in a crouch.

The Mimbres was on him with pantherlike swiftness. The knife streaked out.

Fargo ducked, shifted, dodged.

Hissing in battled anger, the Apache stabbed low. It was a feint. Quick as thought, he arced the blade high, slashing at Fargo's throat.

It was a common trick. A trick Fargo has used. A trick he countered by blocking the blow with his forearm while simultaneously burying his toothpick to the hilt in the warrior's neck. He went for the jugular and he opened it wide.

Spouting scarlet, the Apache skipped backward. He managed only a half dozen steps when his legs buckled and he folded, disbelief writ large on his swarthy features. He tried to speak but all that came out was blood.

The spark of life that animated his eyes faded, and he was dead before he was prone.

Fargo had no time to waste. He grabbed the Henry and swung back on the Ovaro.

The battle was reaching its climax. Most of Grind's hired killers were down.

So were a dozen Apaches.

As Fargo looked on, Jefferson Grind and Fraco broke out of the melee and fled.

Maybe it was the fact they had lost all sense of direction in the fight, or maybe they chose the only way open, or maybe it was simple fear on Grind's part if not on Fraco's, but the pair did not head west, as they had been doing. They galloped madly back the way they had come.

Toward the bend.

Toward Fargo.

They had not noticed him yet. Both were staring back at the Mimbres. No doubt they figured the Apaches would give chase but the warriors were gathering up their wounded and dead and did not come after them.

Wedging the stock to his shoulder, Fargo sighted on Jefferson Grind's sternum. He held his fire, letting them get closer. He wanted to be sure.

Fraco was the first to turn and spot Fargo and the Ovaro. He yelled a warning while at the same time reining sharply to the north.

Jefferson Grind whipped around so fast it was a wonder his neck didn't snap. He brought up his rifle.

Fargo's trigger finger curled. The Henry bucked once, bucked twice, bucked a third time, and the would-be freight king toppled to the ground and was no more.

Forty yards out, Fraco looked back and smirked, confident he would make good his escape. It would take an exceptional marksman to hit him, bent low as he was, and reining right and left.

Fargo put a slug smack in the center of the smirk.

*　　*　　*

That evening the freighters were in fine spirits.

Fargo was filling his tin cup with steaming coffee when three lovelies joined him.

"You didn't think we were done with you, did you?" Cleopatra asked, a twinkle in her eyes.

"I hoped not," Skye Fargo said.

"When you finish that coffee, how about if we go on that walk you promised me?"

Fargo set down the cup. "Why wait?" He took her hand and they walked toward a gap between the wagons.

"Tomorrow night it will be Mavis's turn," Cleo said. "And the night after that, Myrtle wants you again." She grinned and swatted him on the backside. "I hope you are up to it."

"I am always up for it," Fargo told her.

They passed the wagons and were alone in the dark. Cleopatra halted and faced him. "Show me."

LOOKING FORWARD!
**The following is the opening
section from the next novel in the exciting
Trailsman series from Signet:**

**THE TRAILSMAN #323
WYOMING DEATH TRAP**

*Wyoming Territory, 1861—
sometimes you don't know who to trust and you
find yourself trapped in a deadly game.*

Something was wrong.

Skye Fargo came through the narrow mountain pass and looked below to the stage station sprawled across a small, rocky stretch of land. On a fine sunny morning in Wyoming, a stage pulled up in front of the place, there should have been some sign of activity. Even the horses in the rope corral seemed strangely still and quiet. The few scattered outbuildings cast deep morning shadows.

Fargo's lake blue eyes narrowed as he sat his Ovaro stallion and scanned the situation more carefully. For the past two months he'd been working for a Mr. Andrew Lund, the wealthiest man in this part of the Territory.

Not only did Lund own the two largest gold mines, he also owned the largest stagecoach line. Fargo's job was to travel the trouble routes and see if he could stop the robbers who'd been making Lund's life hell. Fargo had been forced to do some killing but so far there had been significant improvement in the safety of the routes. His biggest regret was that despite his efforts, two drivers and a passenger had been killed in one part of the Territory while Fargo had been pulled away to sack a gang in the other.

Fargo knew the man and wife who ran this station for Lund. They were in their sixties, had been farmers until they got too old and too weary to fight off Indians any longer, and ran the cleanest station with the best food anywhere in the entire Lund organization.

Whatever the problem was, it wasn't Indians. Indians weren't quiet unless they were lying in wait. Plus, one of the Indians would have been rounding up the horses in the corral, running them off if not stealing them.

To the west of the station was a line of scrub pine. At the moment a couple of deer were sampling the grass carpeting the thin area of forest.

Fargo walked his Ovaro over to the trees, hiding it in a separate copse of pines. He ran to the denser spread of trees and began working his way in morning shadow to the area behind the station. The scent of pine was sweet and the forest creatures inquisitive as this giant made his way through their kingdom.

Nothing moved in back of the adobe-sided station, either. Empty crates were stacked on one side of the rear door, the other side was empty. There was a window on the empty side.

Fargo moved carefully, crouching down, Colt drawn and ready, working his way to the window on the back wall. The only sounds were those of the soughing mountain winds, the cries of a soaring hawk, and the creaking of pine limbs when the wind came hard.

He ducked below the window, preparing himself for surprise. He might well ease himself up to peer inside and find himself staring at another human being. A damned unfriendly one.

He inched himself up to the window. No face awaited him. What he saw was self-explanatory. In the center of the station four passengers stood together while three masked gunmen went through their bags. A fourth gunman stood to the side, holding a sawed-off shotgun on them.

Fargo didn't see Lem Cantwell, the station manager, at first, but as his eyes searched the large central room inside they spotted a snakelike line of red on the stone floor and traced the line all the way to the bloody white-haired head of an older man. With a dark, ragged hole the size of a baseball on the left side of his head, there was no doubt that he was dead. Fargo didn't see Pauline, Lem's wife. Had the bastards killed her, too?

The first thing he had to do was check his anger. Much as he wanted to go bursting in there now, he'd probably only get himself killed and help nobody.

He forced himself to focus on the job at hand and not the Cantwells.

He crouched down again and duckwalked over to the side of the door. He stood up, slid his hand over to the doorknob and gently began turning it back and forth.

The conversation inside went on without interruption. One of the passengers was a pretty girl and so naturally at least two of the bastards were talking about how they were going to rape her when they were done robbing everybody. A third robber kept threatening the passengers to turn over everything valuable they had on them. He said that anybody caught holding out would be killed. But surely by now the passengers knew that they were to be killed no matter what they said or did.

Nobody had heard Fargo twisting the doorknob back and forth.

He twisted faster, harder, until one of them said: "What the hell's that?"

By now the girl was crying so hard that hearing the doorknob turn was even more difficult. But between her sobs one of the men said: "It's the back door."

"The back door?" another robber said. "Who the hell'd be coming in the back door?" Then: "Lou, you go find out."

"Cover me," Lou said. "This is strange."

Fargo gave the knob a final twist. Then he pressed himself flat against the adobe and waited. The chinking sound of Lou's spurs grew louder the closer he got to the door.

Fargo knew he had only seconds to act.

The door opened, and the brim of a filthy white Stetson poked out of the doorframe. Fargo slapped the hat off Lou's head and just as Lou turned to see who his assailant was—bringing his gun up—Fargo brought his own revolver down so hard on Lou's skull that the scrawny man dropped without another sound. Fargo started dragging him away just as he hit the ground.

Fargo knew that the men inside still had the advantage. Three of them plus a sawed-off shotgun. If he went in there and started shooting he'd do the very thing he hoped to avoid—get the passengers killed.

He heard shouts and threats, and then a couple of the men running to the back door.

But Fargo was still dragging Lou by his long, filthy black hair. Lou was going to have one hell of a headache when he woke up.

On the side of the station Fargo found an empty barrel. He hauled Lou and the barrel in front of the building. By now Lou was conscious, spluttering and cursing. Fargo put his gun to Lou's right temple and said, "Turn the barrel over so you can sit on it and then sit down."

"What the hell you think you're doing? And why the hell'd you have to drag me by my hair, you son of a bitch? You know how much my head hurts?"

Fargo ripped the man's mask off. He was a middle-aged man, with pinched features, a broken nose, a brown walleye on the left. "What's your name?"

The man said nothing. Fargo slapped him hard across the back of the head. "You hear me? What's your name?"

"Clemmons."

"Any of the others named Clemmons?"

Silence again. This time Fargo grabbed a handful of hair and pulled. Clemmons's scream played off the mountains.

Clemmons said, "They're all my brothers."

"I was hoping for that." These days many outlaw gangs were kin of some sort. "Brothers" was the jackpot.

Fargo shouted, "You heard him scream. The next time he screams it'll be because I put a bullet through his head. You want your brother to die?"

The expected response: "You hurt my brother, mister, you're as good as dead."

"That may be, but brother Lou here'll die before I do."

"Help us!" cried one of the passengers.

"I'll tell you how this is going to work," Fargo shouted. The front of the station had a wide door in the center and a small window on the south end. There was no face in the window. "I'm going to give you one minute to let the passengers go. If they don't start coming out, I kill your brother."

"Then we'll kill them."

"Fine. But your brother dies with them."

"He'll kill me, Sam! You don't know him! He already tore out half my hair draggin' me around here!"

"Help us!" the same passenger cried again.

"I want Pauline Cantwell, too."

"If you mean the old woman, she's dead."

Fargo was tempted to kill Lou Clemmons here and now. The Clemmonses would occupy a special place in any hell Fargo designed. But the purpose of using Lou as a hostage was to get the passengers out safe. It was a gamble, Fargo knew. The men inside might just kill them all right now. But they planned to kill them anyway. At least this way there was a chance they'd survive.

"The old lady's dead, just like you're gonna be."

"Goddamn, Sam! Don't make him no madder than he already is!" Lou Clemmons pleaded.

"I'm counting off starting right now, Clemmons. If you don't send them out right away, you'll be burying your brother this morning."

"Listen to him, Sam! Listen to him!"

Fargo could hear them talking. Arguing, really. Finally a new voice shouted: "Don't kill him!"

"Then send out the passengers."

"You son of a bitch," one of them said.

"That won't get you anywhere. Now open the door and send them out."

Fargo's nose detected a warm, sour smell. Lou Clemmons had wet himself. "This isn't right, mister. You'd be killing me in cold blood."

"How'd the Cantwells die in there? I should've killed you already."

Clemmons sucked up tears.

"Ten seconds!" Fargo shouted.

Heavy footsteps inside. Arguing again. The door was pulled back.

A man in a Roman collar and a dark suit came out first. The suit had been splashed with his own vomit. When he reached the ground outside, he flung his arms to the heavens and offered a silent prayer. Then he stumbled toward Fargo.

The second person out was a heavyset woman in a shawl and a gingham dress. She had a hard prairie face. She looked a lot tougher than the minister or, for that matter, Lou Clemmons. She walked straight for Fargo and took her place standing behind him where the minister was.

The girl came third. She wore brown butternuts and a white cotton blouse that hung in shreds. They'd already started to assault her. She didn't seem to notice or care that one of her small fine breasts was exposed. Fargo wondered uncharitably if the minister would faint. She was dazed and lost. The heavyset woman walked to her, took off her shawl and wrapped it around the girl to cover her. She slid her arm around her and then half carried her to a position behind Fargo.

Last came a little elderly man whose face was covered in blood.

What the hell had a little old man said or done to them that caused him to be beaten so severely? His face was a pudding of red blood under which small features could dimly be seen. He wore a green suit soaked with his own gore, and the way he stumbled, Fargo wondered if he could even make it to a position behind him.

The minister hurried to him. He literally picked up the small man in his arms and rushed him back to where the woman and the girl stood. He set him down and immediately began wiping the old man's face with a cloth and soothing him with words. Fargo thought much better of the religious man now.

"Now we want our brother, you bastard!"

"Not going to get him," Fargo said. He angled his head quickly so that the four behind him could hear him. "Head for those trees over there. Get way out of range."

"Oh, shit," Lou Clemmons said, and just after he spoke the words he filled his pants.

"Hurry," Fargo snapped to the four.

He didn't watch them but he heard them walking, running, dragging, scurrying to get out of range any way they could. Now it was just Fargo and the Clemmonses.

"We want our brother. Send him over here."

Fargo pretended not to hear. "I want all three of you to walk out here and throw your guns down. You don't do that, your brother dies right now."

"That ain't what you promised."

"I didn't promise anything. Now do like I say or he's dead."

"Please, Sam! Please!" Lou Clemmons didn't mind fouling himself, apparently, but crying was so unmanly he worked hard at pretending those weren't tears running down his cheeks or trembling in his voice.

"All right. We're coming out."

"One step outside, you throw your guns away or he dies."

"I'm getting goddamned sick of you."

"Feeling's mutual. Now do like I say."

The door squeaked open and two men who had the misfortune of looking pretty much like their brother Lou came out. They'd tossed their masks. There was no point now.

"The guns," Fargo said.

"You're gonna be dead in three minutes."

"Sam, Sam, please don't say that to him," Clemmons whined. "Shit's sake, man, he's got a gun barrel pressed right against my temple."

"The guns."

They sneered and they stalled, but when they heard the hammer pulled back on Fargo's Colt, they pitched their guns a few feet away.

Sun glinted off something metal. Fargo angled his head so he could follow the brightness. A rifle barrel was edging its way into the front window.

"Tell the other one to get out here."

"Sam, Sam, tell Ollie. Tell him he's gonna get me killed."

From inside Ollie bellowed: "I can get a clean shot at him like I said, Sam! I just bust the window and kill him! I got me a rifle!"

"Tell him to get his ass out here. Time the window's broken, you got a dead brother on your hands."

Sam frowned. Fargo figured he'd probably gone along with the idea of suddenly showing a rifle and gunning him down. But now that Sam and his other brother were out here it looked different. Killing Fargo from the window now looked hopeless.

"Get your ass out here like the man says, Ollie."

"But I got a rifle."

"Yeah, and this man's got Lou. Now get your ass out here. I don't want to tell you again."

"Damn you, Sam." Ollie sounded like a very disappointed child. He made a lot of noise slamming against things as he crossed the length of the station to the front door. He stood in the doorway, another Lou Clemmons look-alike except for the meanness quotient. The Good Lord must have filled up his meanness tank full to the brim. "I shoulda let him kill you, Lou. Lettin' him snag you the way he done."

"Just get out here so he'll let me go," Clemmons said.

Ollie spat some of his chaw to the ground and then started walking his way to the others. He walked slowly, hoping to irritate Fargo and show everybody he wasn't afraid. Like too many gunnies he was a ham actor.

"Pitch the rifle."

"Yessir, Commander, sir. I sure wouldn't want to displease you none." He spat again but he pitched the rifle.

If he hadn't taken the next three steps, Fargo wouldn't have been able to guess what Ollie had in mind. But the way he moved, the way his back was arched unnaturally, told Fargo what Ollie intended.

Fortunately for Fargo, Ollie was not only obvious about trying to hide a gun down the back of his Levi's; he was also so hotheaded he couldn't wait for a good chance to use it.

Ollie shouted, "Now!" and flung himself down to the ground. In some ways the moment was pathetic. Ollie had trouble ripping the gun from the back of his jeans, and by the time it saw daylight Fargo had put a bullet straight into the top of his skull. Blood and brain exploded like a fireworks display.

Excerpt from *WYOMING DEATH TRAP*

Fargo had been distracted long enough for the other two to grab their guns. Lou Clemmons screamed, "No! Please no!" Those were his last earthly words. His brothers, attempting to shoot Fargo, killed their brother instead. He fell sideways off the barrel.

By this time Fargo had thrown himself to the ground with a good deal more success than Ollie had. He rolled left, he rolled right, with enough speed to make hitting him difficult. Their shots came in gun-emptying barrages. Rage had made them forget that they had only six bullets apiece, maybe fewer unless they'd reloaded inside.

Fargo shot with more care than either of the remaining brothers. He got Sam in the throat. The man went dramatically, calling out for his mother before he fell to the ground.

The other brother he got twice in the heart. The man's gun went flying into the air. Then he pitched forward, slamming his head on a razor-sharp edge of embedded rock. The fall probably would have killed him without the bullets.

Fargo glanced at Lou Clemmons. He'd been shot twice in the face. He was as much of a mess as station manager Lem Cantwell was inside.

Fargo got to his feet. For long seconds all he could hear were the echoes of all the gunfire; all he could smell and taste was gun smoke. But then the wind came and cleansed the air of the gun smoke and birds replaced the crack of bullets.

He turned to the people he'd ordered out of range. The killings inside the station and out had dulled their eyes and crippled their bodies. They watched him suspiciously, as if he might turn on them, as if this might be a nightmare without end.

But he smiled at them. The heavyset woman, who clutched the girl as if she were her daughter, laughed and said: "It's really over, isn't it?"

"Yeah," Fargo said, "it's really over."